ENTANGLED EMERALD ENCHANTMENTS

ENTANGLED EMERALD ENCHANTMENTS

Carroll Clarke

By the same author

Lockdown Angel

ISBN: 978-94-91868-07-8

©2023

Cover artwork by Stella Brooks-Penrose

SLIDE Books, London/The Hague

Typeset by Steve Lambley Information Design

10 9 8 7 6 5 4 3 2

This book is dedicated with love and gratitude to all those people who have made it possible

You all know who you are

O the mind, mind hath mountains; cliffs of fall
Frightful, sheer, no-man fathomed. Hold them cheap
May who ne'er hung there.

Gerald Manley Hopkins,
'No Worst, There Is None'

TABLE OF CONTENTS

INTRODUCTION

Key Characters and Mask Status

Mark Mobley – unmarried linguist and analyst. Depressive. Intermittent mask wearer.

Jo – gender fluid model, mathematician and linguist. Social isolate. Indifferent to Masks.

Fairy Godfather – high level American Intelligence Agency operative based in Hawaii. Mask adverse.

Ann – housekeeper, middle aged, widowed. Mask wearer if requested by others.

Tom – window cleaner, marital status unknown. Fully masked.

Pat – paramedic, married. Mask free when not working.

Various Policemen and Detectives, aka Scarecrows – intermittent mask wearers.

Parents of Mark Mobley – ineffectual. Mask free.

Anna – Martina's younger half sister. Mask free.

Martina – Enchantress working at AquaCity. Neuro-divergent. Beautiful. Sexually aware and disinhibited. Wearer of Green Glasses. Intermittent mask wearer.

Pat – Psychopharmacologist. Ostensibly neurotypical but questionable. Masked at most times.

Time Frame

Before Covid

Covid Era

Settings

London, Gloucestershire, Hawaii, Slovakia and
Dreams of Djibouti

Chapter One

MARK'S TALE – BEFORE COVID

'The value of things is not the time they last, but the intensity with which they occur. That is why there are unforgettable moments and unique people!'

Fernando Pessoa, *The Book of Disquiet*

Nat King Cole was singing 'Unforgettable' from the radio I could hear in the distance. Today would be unforgettable for me. I began to enter the room cautiously. Not sure what I would find and even less sure if I would know what to do once I had found it. I felt a slight anxiety and yet at the same time a serene sense of peace. The atmosphere was still and slightly chilled. Everything seemed silently static. Nothing moved, neither within the room or even without. It was as if the world had been paused.

I looked out of the window, no birds, no breeze, no rain, nothing. Not even a cloud to disturb the gentle stillness of the translucent pinky grey skies. It seemed as if he had taken everything with him. The air which had managed to remain in the room felt heavily oppressive. I cut through its weight as I allowed my foot to venture across the threshold and then, when my body had followed its desired direction, to stand still. In so doing I had become part of this tableau of frozen abandonment. He was gone. He had left.

I remained in the doorway for as much time as it took for me to recognise what had happened, dismiss my emotions and then accept what I was seeing. When my resigned brain had undertaken all these new demands that were being thrust upon it, I then became able to move forward towards his body. I had shut the door behind me, knowing privacy would always be one of his requirements. We were together alone in this space which he had transformed into his own hallowed sarcophagus.

I had watched enough TV dramas to know that I should not touch anything. But dramas were not real. The tableau I had been forced to reluctantly gate-crash became my only reality. I knew I had to touch him. Not just to ensure that my initial observations were correct but out of a strange sense of respect, care and compassion. This man, who had stilled the world around him, needed me to caress his recently abandoned body. It became an act of benediction, an act of understanding. His leaving the world was an affront to the space around him. The space had been desecrated. The air, the surroundings, the light ... all aspects of natural existence had been affronted by his recently accomplished do-it-yourself exodus. He had shocked the world by leaving it in an untimely fashion. It would take a while for the space around him to regain its composure after such a dramatic trauma. Nat King Cole stopped singing. Silence flooded the room.

My touching him would be the only link between who he had been and where he was now going. It would be an affirmation and acceptance of the wrongness of his departure. Prayers and blessings towards his remains were all that I could do to try to quell the affront caused by his self-inflicted aggression. Forgiveness, compassion and care were the threads linking my world and his. They were necessary for his journey. My presence was a confirmation of his past existence, and my visceral upset and distress, a passport linking this world and the next.

In some way I wanted to try to mitigate the enormity of his transgression. I reached out my hand and placed it gently on the crown of his vacant forehead. The smooth icy coldness reaffirmed to my fingers what my mind had already understood … that he had left. There was no part of him here. He had gone. He was somewhere else.

I gently called through the door to the two people on the other side,

'Please call an ambulance.'

There was a scurry of activity outside the room. I could hear them beginning to argue, though I could not hear their exact words. I knew they did not like each other. Both of them had independently told me of their dislike. Sometimes life is like that. For no obvious reason we can all just take a dislike of another person. Sadly these two were forced to meet at least twice a week and endure their mutual distaste. I began to feel irritated. Knowing the enormity of the scene I was witnessing, it seemed puerile for the two individuals in the hallway to begin an argument within metres of such a devastating catastrophe.

'I'm coming in,' shouted the male voice from the landing. 'I'm coming in because you won't know what to do. You might touch something important. Don't touch anything,' he continued.

My irritation became evident in my raised voice as I replied.

'Don't enter. Just do as I say and call an ambulance now. Stop bickering the pair of you and call an ambulance, then go downstairs, open the front door and wait for the paramedics.'

The voices outside stopped as I heard footsteps moving away from the door towards the staircase. I was thankful that they seemed to be doing as I asked. Soon there was silence. They had both gone downstairs, hopefully to carry out my instructions regarding calling an ambulance.

Sadly, I knew however quickly the ambulance arrived it would still be too late.

I looked around the usually well-ordered room. Nothing seemed out of place. Nothing seemed disturbed. There were no posters or pictures on the walls, apart from a large photograph of a young man. It was a strange photo as someone had obviously stuck a pointed green hat on the subject's head and a cut out of a crocodile sprawled across his neck. It was a very strange image. As I looked closer I noticed someone had written 'Peter Pan Forever' across the body of the crocodile. I had never seen such a strange photograph before. I wonder who the man was who had pride of place in Mark's room.

I then saw a very large lever arch file sitting on the upright chair by the corner sink. It was of funereal colours, black and grey. A single sheet of A4 paper had been sellotaped to the front and the words, 'FOR THE ATTENTION OF SONIA ONLY', written in large black letters diagonally across the paper. I was the Sonia in question. I had been his landlady for nearly ten years, but I hardly knew him. The file had been left for me. His intention had been for me to be the one to discover his body which he had so painstakingly left behind.

I lifted the file and as I did so two envelopes fell to the floor. I picked them up. The first one read 'My Suicide Note' and the second 'For no one else … ONLY SONIA'. I felt a new closeness to this man who had so recently placed me in the position of being both his confidante and his pen pal. I put the second envelope with my name on it in my pocket, returned the file to the chair, and gently teased open the envelope holding the suicide note. It read as follows:

To Sonia and Whoever Else It May Concern. This is the last letter and suicide note from Mark Mobley

Dear Sonia

Please accept my apologies for burdening you with the problem of disposing of my remains. I cannot continue and I have decided to leave before decline becomes decay. I leave with a light heart so please feel no remorse. I have done much in my lifetime.

I want my remains to be cremated at minimal cost and with no memorial service. Please spread my ashes on the top of the beautiful hill which I see from my window every morning and place a death notice in the local paper. I have no living relatives. No individual or organisation may make a valid claim on my estate. I have made no will. It is my wish for my estate to be placed at the disposal of the state. All the necessary information needed I have put in the lever arch file on my chair. You may clear my room as you see fit.

Please do not feel concerned for me. This Lost Boy had decided to return to Never Never Land in a cloud of green dust, where he will fly with his Peter Pan. I will be content. I will be free.

Faithfully and with kind regards

Mark Mobley

I stood for some time, trying to absorb the words he had written. Part of me did not want to accept them. Part of me wanted this all to be a big mistake. Part of me wanted to wake up and realise that I had been having a nightmare. Sadly the rest of me knew what was happening. The rest of me knew I had to deal with the situation in front of me.

Despite being irritated by the two argumentative beings beyond the room, I knew I needed help to manage the situation I was encountering. I called loudly to them again, hoping they were still in ear-shot.

'Open the front door and await the arrival of the ambulance,' were the instructions I found being thrust authoritatively from my mouth and through the closed door.

Out of respect I did not want them anywhere near Mark's body. Mark had been a very private, almost a reclusive individual. I knew he would not have wanted anyone near him. I also felt that the room had now become a sacred space: a sacred space which needed protecting. I wanted them to move as far away from the room as possible. Instructing them to go downstairs and be ready to let the paramedics into the house was my attempt to ensure both privacy and non-interference.

My mind returned to the room. Once again, I moved towards his body. I did not need to touch him a second time. My initial expectations had been confirmed by his coldness. My hands remained idle and compliant at my sides, but my eyes stayed with him, trying to understand what had caused his recent evacuation. His torso was sitting upright, almost erect, and with his head slumped down towards his chest. He must have slipped from the bed and onto the carpet. The bedside cabinet and the wall were supporting him. He could have just been sitting on the floor in preparation to read a book or listen to some music. But no, this body was vacant. This body was recoiled within a puddle of dark red stickiness. This body would not be able to read any book or listen to any music. This body had become unfit for purpose. This body was defunct.

I noticed two CDs on the table. One was a collection of Fado music from Portugal and the second was a song I did not know called 'Lost Boy' by Ruth B. My mind pondered. He had mentioned being a lost boy in his note. He also had that strange photo hanging above his bed stating 'Peter Pan Forever'. I wondered about the significance of the song. Perhaps now, by his transgressions, he really had become a boy who would be lost forever. I would ask Alexa to play the song for me when I returned home. There was a book on the bed. It was entitled *The Book of Disquiet* by Fernando Pessoa. I did not know of the book but I thought that now there would be no 'disquiet'. Quiet was all that was left in this room.

Sometime later, I am not sure how long, I heard an unfamiliar voice call from outside the room.

'Are you alright in there?'

'Yes, I'm fine,' I replied.

No sooner had my reply left the room than the door was being opened. A woman in a paramedic's uniform moved towards me.

'Are you OK?' she asked again.

I was by now becoming a bit bemused. I was now beginning to consider what had happened. I tried to make sense of it. Her concern for me quickly abated as soon as I assured her that I really was OK. She moved away from me towards Mark where another male paramedic, who must have slipped quietly into the room with her, was already attending to the body. He was doing various procedures, to help him establish if any signs of life were discernible. This young paramedic looked at his co-worker and shook his head. Now the three of us shared the knowledge that the body was empty, that he really had gone. We three knew there was nothing we could do. A sort of quiet peace and resignation swirled slowly around the room.

'Come downstairs,' the woman gently directed.

I began to obey her instructions. I picked up the folder, hugged it to my chest and moved towards the door. I moved slowly, not sure of my legs. They seem to have become heavy and not trustworthy. Perhaps I was showing signs of shock. Still clutching the folder to my chest with my left hand, I allowed my right hand to gladly accept the outstretched arm which the male paramedic offered. I left the room and moved gradually towards the stairs. Slowly, very slowly and carefully I descended the carpeted stairwell, eventually arriving in the hallway below. The two paramedics followed me.

We had all left him. Mark, what was left of Mark, was now completely alone. I felt a large sigh leave my body. I knew this day would be imprinted on my memory. This day of intensity, made up of 'unforgettable moments' and 'unique people' was destined to haunt the rest of my consciousness. I would never again be the person who had awoken at seven thirty, to a peaceful morning and a mind as bland as the white Egyptian cotton sheets which had surrounded me.

As I stood in the hallway, supported by the paramedics, I knew my life would never be the same again. Mark and I had now become painfully knotted together as we grappled within our understandings of this world and the next. I closed my eyes and conjured the image of Mark slumped on the floor, his body lifeless and unresponsive. The Mark I knew was now changed.

My thoughts then returned to me. I felt trepidation as I realised that he was not the only one to be consumed by his decision to end his life. I too, had now become part of his aggression. I now knew that, like Mark, I too had become changed forever.

Cogitations

The World Health Organization, 'Suicide', 17 June 2021 states that:

'Stigma, particularly surrounding mental disorders and suicide, means many people thinking of taking their own life or who have attempted suicide are not seeking help and are therefore not getting the help they need.'

'Raising community awareness and breaking down the taboo is important for countries to make progress in preventing suicide.'

The mental health issues surrounding depression and suicide have been greatly affected by the Covid pandemic. Mind, the mental health charity, reported on 17 December 2020 that:

'Mind today reveals new research into men's metal health showing that while some progress has been made, men feel worried or low more regularly than 10 years ago and are consequently twice as likely to feel suicidal.'

'Higher rates of suicide are found in minority communities including gay men' and 'men aged 40-49 have the highest suicide rates in the UK.'

www.mentalhealth.org.uk

The Samaritans, in *The Guardian* (1 September 2020):

> '"Volunteers are telling us that many callers have been worried about losing their job and/or business and their finances, with common themes around not being able to pay rent/mortgage, inability to support the family, and fear of homelessness," Vicki Nash, the head of policy and campaigns at the charity Mind, said. "Not all suicides are mental health-related but many are, and we know that a significant proportion of people who take their own lives have asked for support for their mental health within the last 12 months, which means that services are failing people when they need help the most."'

Sky News correspondent, Jon Graig, 1 April 2022, reporting on items purportedly coming from 10 Downing Street regarding conversion therapy within the LGBT community:

> 'The Government has got itself in a muddle over its pledge to ban conversion therapy. In the Queen's Speech last year ministers said "we will ban conversion therapy to prevent these abhorrent practices, which can cause mental and physical harm. People should be free to be themselves in the UK."'

> Number 10 insisted that there would be legislation in the Queen's Speech due on 10 May 2022. There would be a ban on gay conversion therapy but not transgender conversion therapy.'

> 'The World Health Organisation (WHO) reports that suicide represents half of all male violent deaths worldwide.' www.verywellmind.com

CHAPTER TWO

DISTURBING REVELATIONS – BEFORE COVID

'The unnatural and the strange have a perfume of their own.'

Fernando Pessoa, *The Book of Disquiet*

In the hallway were the two people I had shouted instructions to earlier. One was my housekeeper Ann, a delightful middle-aged woman who would do almost anything for almost anyone. Everyone who lived in this house of multiple occupancy was very fond of her, as was I.

The second person, Tom, was someone I hardly knew. He had moved into the room adjacent to Mark's only a few weeks earlier. He said he was a window cleaner, but somehow, I did not trust him. I don't know whether it was his manner or his voice, or even his look, but I felt uncomfortable. There was something which was just not right. He seemed very self-composed and sure of himself. Nevertheless I felt I did not like him, but rationalised that I would not be seeing much of him so it didn't really matter, so I let him rent the room.

Sadly, Ann too had quickly taken a dislike to Tom. She had been working for me for many years and had never taken a dislike to anyone. She said that Tom was always sneaking around the house and creeping up behind her as she cleaned the rooms. He was always asking her questions about the area and what Mark did for fun.

I reassured her that he was obviously new to our country and was just interested in how we lived and what facilities could be found in Cheltenham. I tried to put her mind at ease, yet at the same time I knew that I was far from comfortable with my own understanding of Tom.

The female paramedic, Pat, introduced herself and continued her directions, suggesting that we all go into the lounge and await the arrival of the police. After seeing my quizzical expression, she explained that it was part of her job to contact the police in situations such as this. I smiled my understanding, adding a diffident nod of the head to reinforce my acceptance of both the situation and her professional position. Obviously, the police would need to be involved.

Ann, Tom and I did as Pat recommended. We moved towards the large lounge. I placed the file and the suicide note, on the oversized coffee table and then lowered myself into one of the velour armchairs, grateful for its support.

A few moments later Pat joined us. She suggested that Ann should make us all a cup of tea. Tom quickly offered to contribute his carton of milk that sat in the fridge in the shared kitchen. Ann left, eager for something to do. Tom apologised and announced that he could not stay as he had work to do. He began to collect various items from around the lounge and started to leave. As he reached the front door two uniformed policemen were just entering and they blocked his way. They explained that as he was witness to what had happened earlier, he would not be able to leave just yet. He was needed. Somewhat irritated at not being able to leave, Tom backed away from the door and rejoined us in the lounge.

The duo of assertive yet polite policemen came into the house. They both moved through the hall and entered into the lounge. The taller of the policemen soon took charge of the situation.

'Please all stay here for the time being,' he requested.

He then left with Pat, and I assumed that they had gone upstairs to Mark's room. We all did as he instructed. No one spoke. A few minutes later, Ann returned to the lounge, with a tray holding mugs of tea, sugar and about six rich tea biscuits placed on a blue and white tea plate. She always brought biscuits to work with her and had obviously decided to share her treats with us all.

We none of us spoke, not even a 'thank you'. Mugs were distributed and biscuits consumed. The policeman who remained with us asked if there was another room available where we could sit. I suggested the dining room or the kitchen. As I did so, Pat and the lead policeman re-entered the lounge. Everyone, except me, was asked to retire to the dining room accompanied by Pat and the second policeman. I remained in the lounge, ready to be questioned. When all the others had left, the lead policeman – he never gave his name – asked me what I knew about Mark and what had happened.

My mind quickly recognised and retrieved the few bits of information I had about Mark. Really there was not a lot. The longest conversation I had ever had with him was when he had first taken a room with me, some ten years earlier. He had been quite open with me then, telling me about his mental breakdown and his relationship with someone at work which had been problematic. The relationship had apparently caused a great deal of trouble, even though he tried to keep it all hidden. The person in question had been called Jo. So, I suppose he/she could have been either sex, or perhaps gender fluid. It seemed that his breakdown was all tied up with his relationship with Jo and his having to leave work. He also said that his parents had forced him to undergo a programme of conversion therapy. I did not know what he meant by this sort of therapy but I also felt that I did not know him well enough to ask him what it was. So really there was very little I knew.

I considered the information that I could immediately muster about Mark. It really had nothing to do with the current situation. It was all ten years ago. I would not tell the policeman about it. All that was needed at the moment, was an overview of what was happening now. I inhaled, looking at the expectant officer as I began.

'Well. I suppose it's best if I start at the beginning of this week. Ann, my housekeeper visits the house to clean and change the bed linen etcetera, every Tuesday and Friday. All the bedrooms are unlocked, but each door has a small bolt which can be pulled across from the inside if anyone is sleeping or wants privacy. Usually, five people live here together but as I am intending to sell the house most tenants have already left. Only Mark and Tom, who you saw earlier, are currently living here. Anyway, on Tuesday, Ann told me that she had been unable to get into Mark's bedroom as the bolt had been pulled. This was unusual. Mark has had a room with us for about ten years. He always allowed access to his room and, on Tuesdays, he would organise the re-cycling ready for collection on Wednesdays. Ann had been concerned. I had suggested that maybe he was feeling a bit off and needed a lie in. Anyway, today, Friday morning, when Ann arrived at nine a.m. as usual, his bedroom was still locked from the inside and the re-cycling had not been put out. Ann was now even more concerned. Tom was in the shared kitchen and according to Ann, he said he'd get his window cleaning ladders and look through Mark's window. It was difficult to put the ladder up against the window because the branches of a large rowan tree blocked his way. But he managed. Then both he and Ann quickly called me. Tom had managed to look through the window and had seen Mark slouched on the floor. I came straight away. I only live round the corner. I asked Tom, who looks strong and has big feet, to kick the door open. This was done. The tiny bolt on the door was easily sprung. I was the only one to enter the room. I only touched Mark's forehead. I found a file addressed to me on his chair with the suicide note. I read the note and then brought the file downstairs with me, which as you can see, I have put on the coffee table. When I realised what had happened, I got Ann and Tom to call the paramedics and they called you and … well … here we all are.'

The policeman thanked me and asked me to join the others in the dining room. I remained in the dining room for the next two hours whilst statements were being made by Ann and Tom. There was considerable movement in the hallway as people in white hazmat suits and boots arrived, presumably to remove the body and to clear the room of anything contaminated by blood or chemicals. There had previously been problems with chemicals in Salisbury so I realised that extra precautions were being taken.

By now I had begun to get slightly emotional. I told Pat that I had chatted to Mark on Monday and that he had seemed OK. I could not understand why he had decided to take his own life; he had seemed quite happy and contented. Her reply was informative. Apparently, her brother, of only thirty-three years, had taken his life. She said that in the days and weeks before he executed his plan, he too had seemed quite happy. She explained that often it seems that once an individual had decided that they are going to leave this world, they become quite resigned and contented, just awaiting the time for their self-inflicted departure.

It was strange, but the police seemed to be particularly interested in Tom. I wondered if Ann had mentioned anything about his inquisitive behaviour to them. They interviewed him twice and then came and asked me what I knew about him. I informed them that he had not been with us long and that I really had nothing to do with him. The only information I would have would be his last address and the reference letter he had provided. Perhaps the police had picked up the questionable vibes that I had experienced when I first met him. I began to go into amateur detective mode, thinking to myself, 'or maybe because he was the person who looked through the window and discovered the body'. Whatever they thought, the police would not let him leave to go to work. They asked me if I would let them have a copy of his reference and his previous address. I said that I would do so when I returned home.

After we had all been individually questioned once, I had to return to the lounge again for further interrogation by the lead policeman. He had read the suicide note and as I entered the room, he was looking at Mark's file, which I had previously placed on the coffee table. He asked me to take a seat and explained that he still had some unanswered questions for me. I was happy to oblige.

His first question was regarding Mark's holidays. I replied that Mark enjoyed painting and that he would tell me that he took painting courses in Paris about three or four times a year. He would be gone for about two or three weeks at a time. It became quite a joke with Ann the housekeeper, as she would see the artwork he was producing, drying in his room. She said that his paintings seemed to be getting worse rather than improving. She thought he must have been wasting his money on art courses in Paris. She was not a Picasso fan, indeed she hated any abstraction. Constable was her painter of preference. I think Constable was the only painter she knew. For my part, I had not seen much of Mark's work but the few 'masterpieces' I had viewed, certainly left a lot to be desired in relation to shape, form and even colour. His work appeared deformed and his colours were always murky. Most of his paintings had been still life compositions. I pondered that now, his final act had also been involved in stilling a life, his life. I considered that a psychologist would have found his strange artistic endeavours interesting.

The policeman also asked how long and how well I had known Mark. I felt quite embarrassed to admit that I had known him nearly ten years, but that I really knew nothing of his life. He had arrived looking for a room when he was out of work. He told me that he had previously worked at the British Government Intelligence Agency HQ. He said that a nervous breakdown and spasmodic bouts of depression meant that he had been forced to leave his position and seek alternative work. He had taken the room, but although he was not working, he had not applied for any housing benefit. I thought this strange at the time, but when I suggested that he should apply he said he did not want to. He mentioned that he did not want to be a strain on the system.

I thought this sentiment was admirable. Most people would grab what they felt they were entitled to. He did not.

Basically, that was all I knew about him. Not a great deal you may think for someone you have known for nearly ten years, but Mark was a very private and closed individual. Disclosure was a word I don't think he understood. He rarely chatted or made conversation. His room held very little. He had no computers or even a TV. He did have an old fashioned radio, which could also take compact discs.

Ann would tell me that she often wondered what he did in his room. She did tell me that he had a mobile phone. She had not actually seen it but he left the charger in the socket at all times, so she knew he had a phone. There were only ever a couple of books in his room at any one time. *The Book of Disquiet*, which I had noticed, was always by his bedside, usually with a paperback thriller placed on top of it. Ann said that he would read the thriller and then discard it to the bin, placing another one on his bedside table in readiness to read. His painting seemed to be his only hobby. Ann had told me that his room was always immaculate. He never had visitors, never spoke of any family or girlfriends. She never had to worry about spilt paint or splashed walls. Everything was always immaculate. He led a very lonely, even peculiar existence. I was reminded of the Simon and Garfunkel song, 'He Was a Most Peculiar Man'.

Ann had also said that she knew he frequently visited one of the cafés in the town centre where they had computers you could use. She had a part time job in the grocers opposite the café and had seen him regularly sitting at one of the computers. She had told me that she wondered why he had not bought his own computer, as he seemed so keen to use the ones in the café. I thought that perhaps he could not afford one of his own. In all the years that I had known him, he had never worked or claimed any benefits, but also, he had never missed paying his rent. I wondered, maybe his family were supporting him, but he never spoke of them. I did not give it anymore thought. I got my rent, and his finances were nothing to do with me. They were not my concern.

I was generally chatting and feeding the limited information about Mark's life to the policeman when suddenly, he looked slightly agitated and confused. He asked me again about the holidays Mark had taken. I made the same reply as I had made earlier, saying that Mark took frequent painting holidays in France.

'But look at this,' he said, showing me Mark's passport, which he had extracted from within the file.

I looked in amazement. Stamps from America, Kurdistan, Uzbekistan, Afghanistan, Russia, Poland, and Ukraine covered the pages. I took the passport and flicked through it. I thought it all very strange. Why had he visited so many strange sounding countries? On seeing the final page I was amazed. I could not believe what I saw.

The last page of every passport holds a section entitled,

EMERGENCIES

The holder should insert below particulars of two relatives or friends who may be contacted in the event of an accident

On this page I saw my name and address printed in black ink, not once but twice. There were spaces for two relatives and friends. He had put my name and address twice. Did he have no one else whose name he could use? Why had he put me? I was not a relative. I was not even a friend. There was no section for 'Landlady'. He had never asked me, and I really did not know him.

'Why would he put me?' I asked the expectant policeman.

We both then began to look through the file. Curiosity and disbelief had made us allies.

The file was full. There were statements from three large High Street banks, showing hundreds of thousands of pounds locked in deposit accounts and numerous papers referring to investment bonds. I just could not understand why Mark was living in my house of multiple occupancy, when he obviously had so much money. He could have bought his own house and still had money to spare. It was all starting to look very mysterious. What was going on?

The lead policeman had been sharing too much with me … we had been inquisitors together, but he suddenly retreated into his professional persona and told me that we should not look at anything else or even repeat what we had been discussing. He asked me to stay in the lounge and to talk to no one. As he left the room he looked back and asked if I had a mobile phone. I said 'yes'.

'Well please do not use it,' was his response.

He left the room clutching the file, only to return a few minutes later, saying that he was being taken off the case and that other plain clothes colleagues would be arriving. He asked me to stay in the lounge and await their arrival. After saying 'goodbye' he quickly left the building.

I was alone, wondering what would happen next. Why was he being removed from the case? Why was there a case? Surely the suicide note was clear. I noticed that he had not only removed the file but the passport as well. I was still confused. Why had Mark listed me in his passport and why had he visited all those far-flung countries? I began wondering what on earth Mark had been getting up to when he took his so called 'holidays to France'. All I could do was to sit and wait.

I sat, looking out of the window. I blinked to try to gain clarity as a small tear fell from the corner of my eye. Everything seemed so disturbing and bewildering. Gradually, my upset mind began to accept that clarity was something I would not find easily. Confusion was pervasive. Little did I realise how long my current confusion would remain with me, or how much it would disturb my future reality.

CHAPTER THREE

MYSTERIOUS CONNECTIONS

'The difference between him and the other boys at such a time was that they knew it was make-believe, while to him make-believe and time were exactly the same thing.'

JM Barrie, *Peter Pan*

We all create our own realities, and within our creations we need a sprinkling of delight and a glimpse of wonder, a touch of make-believe. I wondered what reality Mark had conceived.

I continued to look out of the lounge window. The green freshness and the simplicity of the blue skies and transient clouds gave me some comfort. To an onlooker, I would have appeared quite serene and calm, but there was a hushed turbulence stirring inside me.

I had planned my day earlier in the week. I usually knew exactly what I intended to do each day. I believed in the maxim 'failing to plan means planning to fail'. I would plan the night before and thus know exactly what was required of me upon awakening in the morning. I did not like leaving things to chance, and I certainly did not like being hi-jacked by my housekeeper in order to break into a bedsit and find a dead body. This day had not been earmarked for 'dead body discovery', but rather for shopping, soup making and weeding.

I watched the gentle garden scene suddenly become invaded by movement. I looked intently. The two original policemen had left the house and were now standing in the front garden, talking underneath the rowan tree. They appeared to be quite agitated. I watched their facial expressions and gesticulations. They seemed concerned and worried, and they continued to talk earnestly for about ten minutes. They then moved towards the wall and picked up a trunk of wood. It was about ten inches tall and seven inches across. As they examined it I could see that it had been hollowed out. They removed what looked like a small camera from its hollowed out middle. Who would have put a camera at the house? What was going on? At the same time there were paramedics in white hazmat coveralls rushing backwards and forwards between the house and two large white vans which were parked on the driveway. Things were becoming rather strange.

I also noticed a few of the neighbours standing on the pavement on the opposite side of the road. They were watching all the activity. The house had become a scene of public interest. The neighbours did not seem to be talking or asking questions. They were just mute observers, maybe confused observers. The white hazmat suits gave the scene a sinister air, almost like something from a science fiction movie. Had the road been invaded by aliens? Was a spaceship about to land? Were the people in the house dangerous? Who had placed a camera hidden in a tree trunk under the grape vine? I wondered what the inquisitive neighbours thought was going on.

I had received letters in the past from one man who lived a few houses away. He, in his detached suburban smugness, had suggested that I should not let the house to undesirables.

I almost retched at the vitriol which leapt out of the envelope along with his handwritten missive. Yet another example of man's inhumanity to man. He appeared to consider himself superior just because he owned his own house and had managed to secure a life without invasion by any mental or physical challenges, or even financial hardships. I considered the various tenants I had known over the years. All had been worthwhile, sensitive and considerate individuals, who had found life, for whatever reason, mental, financial, or physical, difficult. They had to manage overcoming their particular obstacles and find a way to live as productively as they could. Surely this required, indeed almost demanded, respect rather than rejection. I usually quietly admired my tenants. I knew at some deep level that I would have been found to be profoundly lacking if I had had to deal with some of the dilemmas which they had experienced in the past or indeed were still encountering. The man had added after his signature 'Chair of the Residents Association and a long respected member of the community'. I wondered how many residents would agree with his prejudices and how many did in fact respect him. I decided to show my particular disrespect by not answering his letter. I just ignored the letter, and made a mental decision that in future I would simply just ignore him too. I wondered if women like me had a limited amount of smiles within them. Science had told me that I had a limited amount of eggs to aid the continuation of the species. I did not want to risk wasting smiles if they were limited. Just imagine reaching the menopause only to find that you had run out of smiles too! In future if I saw the prejudiced and contaminated Chair on the street I would not smile. He would be ignored. I would not even waste a smile on him.

My thoughts returned to the inquisitive neighbours, as their minds reached out from across the road, towards the activity before them. Had I not been so embroiled in the dramatics of the situation myself I might have gone over to ask them what they understood was happening. However, I was too stressed and upset to consider such an action. I felt for the neighbours but selfishly I did nothing to try to quell their anxieties.

I resumed looking from the window. Beyond the grape vine which clung to the front Cotswold stone wall, a large black car slowed down and stopped in front of the house. Three men got out of the vehicle and moved laboriously towards the policemen in the garden. There were now five men standing in a circle on the grass. They all stood talking for about five minutes, after which, the two original policemen got in their white and yellow panda car and drove away. They did not say goodbye and I never saw them again.

My thoughts returned to the neighbours. The group had grown from five to twelve. It seemed the arrival of more police acted as a magnet for further attention and discussion. I again wondered what the neighbours were thinking. I doubted that they would have considered a death by suicide to be the cause of all the activity. Indeed, I suspected that most ordinary disturbances would have been dealt with quietly and calmly. Things did seem to be more dramatic and intriguing now that the new police and extra neighbours had joined the activity.

I closed my eyes and felt concern. Everything seemed to be getting more confusing and more demanding. I did not want to be involved. I felt slight frustration and annoyance. I did not want to be chosen by Mark. I did not want Mark to kill himself. I wished that it was still yesterday. I did not like the way today was panning out. Self-serving thoughts rambled around my head. I wanted to go shopping, make some soup and finally attack the weeds which were determined to strangle my peonies.

A few minutes later, there was a knock on the lounge door and two of the new plain clothed officers entered and introduced themselves, saying they were the detectives who would be taking over the investigation. I had expected that plain clothed officers would look as smart as the previous uniformed policemen. These two looked shabby and unkempt, as if they had obtained their plain clothes costumes from a down-market jumble sale. Their suits were shiny at the elbows and knees, whilst their white shirts were tinged with grey and looked crumpled and unironed. They were both very lanky and thin, with sallow skin and receding hairlines. I felt sorry for the men. My sexist viewpoint flooded my thoughts. They both looked unloved. Obviously, they did not have a mum or a wife to get them ready for the day ahead. I expected that maybe as children they had not had their hankies checked or apples placed in their hands as they left for school. They looked like relatives of the scarecrow from the *Wizard of Oz*. Like scarecrow siblings, trying to look tidy as they were getting ready to go to a dance or a party. The third plain clothed officer then joined us. He was short, and overweight and his clothes were crisp and immaculate. Rather than looking like a scarecrow, he was more of a peacock. The peacock explained that he would have to ask me further questions. The twin scarecrows left the room whilst he turned his attention towards me, requesting that I sit down and make myself comfortable.

Everything that I had discussed with the first policeman was discussed again. The questions were almost identical.

I assumed that the other two detectives were interviewing Ann and Tom in the other rooms. My new detective took copious notes. For over an hour, Ann, Tom and I were interviewed and not allowed to talk to each other. We were kept in separate rooms. Me in the lounge, Tom in the dining room and Ann, appropriately in the kitchen.

The newly arrived detectives were distant. Not open and informative like the original two men. I had been in the lounge for what seemed like hours. I was beginning to feel stressed and uncomfortable. Why was everything taking so long? I did not understand what was going on. I knew that Mark's body had been removed during the late morning. His room had been sealed. Pat had handed me the name of a specialist cleaning company which dealt with thorough cleaning. Professional cleansing was necessary after any deaths which could possibly involve contamination and blood spillage.

The police officers had interviewed us all numerous times and we had been totally co-operative. They had all the information that we could give them. It seemed to me that these new detectives were just keeping us in the house in case they could think of yet another question which needed answering, or some new line of enquiry which they had failed to consider before. Or maybe they just liked Ann's copious mugs of tea which she kept producing during her kitchen incarceration. Whatever the reason, my calm patience was beginning to show signs of fracture. I was fed up, bored, cold, hungry and tired. My usual pleasant accommodating self was on the verge of leaving my body, to be replaced by … thankfully I never found out who or what the replacement was going to be, as the others entered the room. The two scarecrows, plus Ann and Tom found seats at the request of my peacock. We were now all together in the lounge, and all looking rather the worse for wear.

The niceties of the morning were forgotten. Our social politeness was evaporating as our tiredness increased. Our plain clothed detectives were not as forthright as our chatty morning policemen, nor as considerate. No more offers of tea or biscuits. No smiles or asking if we were alright. It all seemed very serious and clinical, almost as if it was our fault that the detectives were having to work today. Had we taken greater care of Mark there would have been no need for any of the apparent trouble and investigation. Personally, I was beginning to feel almost guilty, well perhaps not guilty but at least responsible. After all, it was my house and I felt that I did have some sort of duty of care for my tenants. Perhaps if I had been more vigilant this might not have happened? I suppose anyone hearing of a death by suicide would wonder if they could have done anything to prevent it.

As the day progressed my initial concern and sadness was being replaced by annoyance and indignation. Why were these detectives treating us like the enemy? We had all tried to help. We had all been through a great deal. Encountering a death by suicide was a harrowing and demanding experience. These detectives seemed more interested in treating us as criminal informants, rather than seeing us as ordinary helpful people who had got mixed up in a difficult and distressing experience.

I had enough energy to try to understand what was happening; to consider that maybe detectives have to deal with such difficult cases every day. Such a plethora of sadness and death could make any person become hardened to their work. I looked at my two unkempt scarecrows sitting by my immaculate peacock and wondered at their mental states. They would have to be strong. They would have to consider those near to the crime to be in some way, potential suspects. But surely Mark's death would have had nothing to do with anybody else? Surely it was an open and shut case. Maybe they just had to be inquisitive and distant as part of their professional camouflage? I was tired. I did not want to try to work out the internal machinations of detectives, even scarecrow detectives. In my weary mind I forgave them their apparent callousness.

Yet again my thoughts became self-serving. I just wanted to go home, have some food, and go to bed. I was hungry and tired. I announced this to everyone in the room. Eventually the lead detective said we could leave the house and go home. It was now early evening. We three had been at the house for most of the day, which was debilitating enough, but we had the added pressures of Mark's death and lack of food. Six biscuits between us all could not be deemed adequate food for the day. Trying to think positively I considered that my demanding day could also be viewed as part of my ongoing diet regime. But I knew it was not a time to diet. My body needed food. My head was assimilating the day but my body was rebelling. The emotional stress we had expelled meant that we needed sustenance, rest and relaxation.

Grateful to be released, we moved into the hall and towards the front door. Ann and Tom slowly exited the house and left straight away. I mustered the energy to wave them goodbye. Ann lived two streets away and she had offered to put Tom up for a few days. She had a spare bedroom at her house and on occasions she would let it out to friends or family, and at times even to our dethroned Chair's 'undesirables'.

Previously the police had told us that we would not be able to enter the house again as it was being classified as a crime scene. They had allowed Tom to go into his room and take some clothes and toiletries. He had to leave most of his stuff, including his ladders and window cleaning gear in the garage. He was furious, arguing that he needed his ladders etcetera for his business and that he would lose a great deal of money if he could not work. His pleas fell on deaf ears. The detectives did not seem to have ears when it came to requests, only ears for statements and answers to their questions.

To ensure that we did not enter the house again we had to relinquish our keys. The defiant part of my existence smiled as I considered that I had three other keys back in my home key safe, which I could easily use in order to scupper the detective's plans. These detectives were not as bright as they should be. They should have asked me if I had any other keys. I felt like a smug schoolgirl who has just proved she is able to outsmart a teacher and find a way to stay in the building during a wet playtime. My delight in my cleverness was crushed when I heard one of the detectives talking to the policeman who had just arrived. This new uniformed office was going to remain at the scene. The crime scene would be guarded, just like on the movies. I would not be able to use my keys after all. These detectives were smart.

I was about to leave and head for home, when I realised that I had left my handbag in the lounge. I went back to get it. As I picked it up from the floor, I discovered a credit card case lying beside it. The credit card case had nothing to do with me. It was not mine. The case must have fallen out of Mark's file when the morning policeman and I were originally looking at the passport. I retrieved the case and opened it. I was amazed. It was not a credit card case. There were two cards inside, both with Mark's photo.

I looked at the first card. Below the photo and Mark's name were the initials AIA, namely the American Intelligence Agency, with an expiry date of the following year. The second card was one I had seen many times before. It was a current card for the British Government Intelligence Agency. I recognised the Government Intelligence Agency card so easily because previously I had had a security guard who worked there lodging with me. He wore the identification badge with pride, but he had glued a picture of a monkey face on top of his own photograph. He would laugh saying that he had worn the identity badge for eight months, it was checked twice daily as he entered and left the building, but nobody ever noticed the monkey face! So much for security and identification at one of our most prestigious and security conscious venues. I knew that there had been a long history of co-operation between the UK and the USA intelligence services. I was gradually seeing Mark in a different light. I seemed to be seeing him from the inside out rather than from the outside in. I also knew that I would have to share what I had discovered with the detectives.

I carefully stepped into the hall where the three plain clothed officers were talking, impatiently waiting for me to get my bag. I handed the card to the nearest fellow. He looked with disbelief, showed it to the other two and then returned his gaze to me. He told me that the cards and the file would have to be given to the coroner. I asked if I could keep the suicide note which had been addressed to me personally. His reply was negative. He also told me that I should just ignore the fact that I had seen the cards. I should forget everything, go home, have some food and rest. He added, in a sterner voice, that I should not discuss anything about the investigation with anyone. It was all to be kept quiet.

Previously Ann, Tom and I had been asked about our telephone numbers and addresses. The lead detective had told us that we would be contacted at home if they needed any further information. All the ends regarding our involvement seemed to be being tied up. I felt happy to be able to leave and return to my undramatic ordinary life.

The three detectives and I moved out of the house and into the front garden. I had previously given my house key to the peacock. I left, but part of my consciousness remained. My curiosity was primed. My thoughts returned to the lounge and the file, but more importantly to the cards I had discovered. I knew that Mark had worked at the British Government Intelligence Agency but now it seemed he was also a current member of the American Intelligence Agency. I had watched enough movies to know that this particular agency was involved in collecting and analysing intelligence in order to aid national security and pre-empt terrorist threats. My life seemed to be entering a period of dramatic uncertainty. I had so many questions and concerns radiating around my head that I thought I might get one of my occasional headaches. It was all becoming a bit too much.

One of my immediate considerations was that I now understood that I knew nothing about the man I had touched so reverently earlier in the day. My previous innocent concern and compassion had now become contaminated by curiosity. Who was this man who had lived with me for nearly ten years and why had he ended his life?

I returned home, made myself a cup of coffee and a sandwich, then I sat in my lounge, waiting for the trials of the day to leave me. I ate the sandwich, drank the coffee and soon fell asleep. On awakening, I went to my study and opened my file cabinet. I would keep a file on each one of my tenants. There was nothing particularly exciting or informative in any of the files, just previous addresses and letters of introduction or references. Sometimes there would be notes the tenants had sent to me or notes that I would make about any points of interest, like how many children they had, or previous jobs and qualifications. I kept most things.

I looked at Mark's file. It was thin. Nothing important. An excellent reference from the Government Intelligence Agency stating how sorry they were that he had had to leave. A previous letter from a landlady saying he was a delightful tenant. There was also one side of A4 in my handwriting. I had obviously scribbled these notes when he had moved in.

'A friendly man. Worked Government Intelligence Agency. Left due to depression and a mental break-down. Said his breakdown was due to an emotional breakup with someone called Jo. Seems OK now. Says he just wants to be quiet and paint. NB Warn Ann to watch out for paint stains in his room.'

Considering the two identity cards I had found it now seemed that he had not left the Government Intelligence Agency but was still employed. Also, that he was a member of the American Intelligence Agency too. I wondered about his depression. It's sad but when you discover that a person had lied to you about one thing you then begin to question everything else that they have told you. He did seem upset when he had originally arrived looking for accommodation. I felt that perhaps the story of the breakdown and the depression had been true. I returned to the lounge and sat in my chair. My mind was full of thoughts about Mark's previous life. Why had he lied about his job? How long he had worked for the American Intelligence Agency? Why had he listed me on his passport? Everything seemed to revolve around this Jo person. I wondered, who is this Jo and did Jo have something to do with Mark's death?

The day and all the activity had been gruelling. My concerns regarding Jo would have to wait. I needed rest and calm. I would ask Alexa to play music which would slow my pulse and decrease the levels of stress hormones that had been rushing around my body all day. I had heard about 'pink noise', which would encourage deep sleep. I asked Alexa to play 'pink noise'. She started playing Pink Floyd 'Another Brick in the Wall'. 'Oh no, that would not help me sleep. Stop Alexa!' I repeated my instructions, and more clearly, thinking that perhaps she did not know about 'pink noise'. To my amazement she did. I found myself listening to a strange mélange of screeches that she said would aid babies sleeping. Not being a baby I knew such pink noise would not help me. It was dreadful, so I told her to play classical piano. That would do the trick for me. I climbed the stairs to bed. Sleep was all I needed. Soon my heavy breathing accompanied Lang Lang playing Debussy's prelude, 'La Fille aux Cheveux de Lin' (The Girl with the Flaxen Hair). Peace ruled. Though I must admit that I am sure my subconscious was still worrying about all those dear babies who were being forced to listen to pink noise, by trendy yet misguided parents!

Sleep would offer me the escape I so desperately needed. Sleep would allow me to absorb the demands of today and heal. Tomorrow would be a different day. I hoped tomorrow would hold no contaminations of today. I had not enjoyed today. I assured myself that tomorrow would be better. My heavy breathing continued as I sank into sleep.

CHAPTER FOUR

CREMATION AND CONFUSION

'Never say goodbye because goodbye means going away and going away means forgetting.'

JM Barrie, *Peter Pan*

I had said my sad goodbyes to Mark when I had touched his body. I hoped my sleep would have soothed my mind and helped me to forget the pain and confusion of yesterday.

Nevertheless, I had still awoken muddled, wondering what was going on. I had overslept and all I could hear was the sound of my front doorbell being rung again and again. Someone wanted me up. Someone wanted to see me. I quickly got out of bed, donned my dressing gown and slippers and I headed for the stairs.

'Hold on,' I thought, 'Hold on, you do not want to fall.'

I carefully made my way down the stairs and into the hall. I could see shadows through the glass window in my front door. The shadows were trying to hide the sunlight which radiated into my hall. Shadows are no opponent to sunlight. Thankfully the sunlight won the battle, and I opened the door to its warmth and vigour.

Sadly, whilst dismissing the shadows, the sunlight had not been able to dismiss the two detective scarecrows who had caused them. They stood before me. My experiences of yesterday came flooding back into my mind.

'Oh no, not more questions,' went through my head.

I heard my voice politely asking if I could be of any help and would they like to come in.

A few moments later we three were ensconced in my lounge. Two scarecrows and one half awake woman in an over washed dressing gown. The one thing we all had in common was straw-like unkempt hair. Not a pretty trio.

The night did not seem to have treated the scarecrows well. Their behaviour seemed to have deteriorated and their accusatory tones increased. I felt distressed and alarmed as they fired more questions at me. Most of the questions were yet again more repeats of the ones I had answered already, but now they seemed to include a peppering of things I knew absolutely nothing about. Things I would not have considered to have anything to do with Mark, me or even most people living in Cheltenham. Had I visited Russia or Ukraine? Who did I stay with when I stayed in Slovakia? What was my political allegiance? Who was Olga? Actually that's a lie. They did not ask me 'Who was Olga?' … that's just me getting carried away in my wonderings! Anyway, as I became more awake, I realised that their questioning showed that they had been checking up on me since our last meeting. They had obviously found out a great deal about me and my trips abroad. I also realised that they suspected that I had not been telling them the truth when I said that I hardly knew Mark.

I sank into my chair, feeling dejected and concerned. How can people not believe others? I never think people are lying to me. Why should they? I wanted to just say openly that they need not fear for I would not lie to them. I looked at their scarecrow faces and realised they just would not believe me. So, my only option was to try to stay within their line of questioning and answer as best I could.

I sat up, smiled and began to offer my open, honest replies. Then suddenly I became aware that I was not as honest as I made out to be. I had conned even myself. Suddenly I remembered all the information about Mark which I had shelved, thinking it was not relevant to his suicide. I sank back into my chair again. These scarecrows knew me better than I knew myself.

I decided to come clean. I decided to explain the reasons for my withholding information.

'I failed to tell you about one aspect of Mark's life. I just thought it was not relevant to your inquiry, but maybe it is? He told me that he had a mental breakdown just before he took the bedsit with me. He had been in a difficult relationship with someone called Jo. I think he felt that Jo was the reason for his breakdown and his subsequent periods of depression. Sorry I did not mention this yesterday, I just thought it not to be important.'

'Let us decide what is and isn't important. That is our job,' was the cold reply.

The atmosphere became clinical. I felt guilty and accused. I did not like being put in my place by anyone, let alone scarecrows. The questioning continued.

Usually I would offer most visitors, tea or coffee. My generosity would extend to chocolate biscuits if I had not already eaten them all. Chocolate biscuits have a limited life span in my house. But I offered nothing. I was pleased when the words 'That will be all for now' hit my ears as the two scarecrows got up and headed for the front door. They had gone.

I moved into the hall and checked that they had closed the front door, then I headed for the shower. I needed cleansing, both physically and metaphorically. I wanted to rid myself of the whole experience. I wanted to return to my pleasant, acceptable persona.

Whilst questioning me, my two detectives had caused me to question myself. Their suspicious minds had infected my mind. I knew I was not as open and honest as I had previously thought I was. I was muddled and confused. Where had my thoughts re Olga come from? Was there really someone called Olga? What was going on? Why was I so mixed up? It was as if they knew me better than I knew myself. I continued washing and scrubbing with extra vim, trying to obliterate any contamination of my established, yet smugly self-righteous understanding of who I was.

Eventually I was ready to greet the day. I got on with my usual tasks. Breakfast, listening to the news, feeding the birds, checking the mail. Life, boring life, continued. I received and made various phone calls. I had to deal with organising the cleaning of Mark's house too. I had to check that Ann and Tom were OK. I had bills to pay and orders to make.

Honouring the requests made by Mark in his suicide note dominated my thoughts. I put a notice in the local paper and contacted the undertakers regarding the cremation. Gradually the detective's visit faded, washed away by the necessities of living. I was almost back to being my old self again. I breathed a sigh of relief.

The phone rang just as I congratulated myself that I had accomplished most of the tasks I had set for the day. I heard a pleasant voice say,

'Good afternoon. I am the coroner dealing with the affairs of Mr. Mark Mobley.'

The conversation continued in a pleasing and supportive manner. Obviously, the scarecrows had not told the coroner that I could not be trusted and that I might be withholding information. The coroner asked about the cremation, saying that he would be attending. He asked if I was well, saying that it must have all been a shock for me. At last, someone was considering my feelings. I warmed to this man on the end of the phone.

Time passed. I was pleased that the scarecrows did not return. All my future communications seemed to come through the coroner.

I began organising the things Mark had requested. I did a mental check list. A Death Notice had been put in the local paper. A date for the cremation had been arranged and advertised in the paper too. I requested a copy of the suicide note from the coroner. My name had been put at the top of the note. I wanted to read it again. It was precious. It was the last thing he had written, and it had been written to me. I felt special and obliged to retain the note. Everything seemed to be sorting itself out. Gradually life was returning to its pre-suicide normality. Days passed.

The following week the coroner rang me to check if I was OK. He was a kind man. He said he would be attending the cremation as he did not think many people would attend. I had previously decided not to go. His thoughtful comments made me feel guilty. I told him I would go too. When I had put the phone down to him I rang Ann, telling her about the cremation. She too wanted to go. We decided to go together.

The day of the cremation arrived. Ann walked to my house, and we drove to the crematorium in my car. The cemetery grounds looked beautiful. Trees surrounded by a confetti of pink and white petals were everywhere and the grass had just been cut. We entered the building, being directed by one of the undertakers. Mark's service was to be taken in the small chapel on the right.

We sat and were soon joined by a man who introduced himself as the coroner. He looked as kind as he had sounded. I liked this man. The three of us awaited the arrival of the coffin. A strange dirge resonated around the cold chapel. My thoughts became wicked as I wondered why the chapel should be so cold. I would have expected a crematorium to be heated! I quickly stopped my irreligious thinking, hoping nobody else was having similar thoughts. The dismal dirge was disturbed by two women entering the chapel talking loudly to each other. We three turned. The women sat behind us and quickly explained that they had known Mark from the local art classes. They did not know him well, but they felt they should come to his funeral. I felt grateful for their consideration towards Mark. I saw the hearing aids they were both wearing. Their noisy entrance was now understood.

A loud 'Oh it's you' emanated from the taller of the two women when she saw Ann. They obviously knew each other. I had always understood that Ann was well known in the area. She seemed to know everyone. She had previously worked in the local laundromat. She seemed not only to know everyone but also to know much about their dirty linen!

The music stopped and everyone became hushed. Two tall men dressed in dark suits and even darker expressions entered and sat across the aisle. The coffin was carried in. A priest welcomed everyone, and after reading from the Bible he said a few words of comfort, supposedly support-ing those of us left behind. The curtains opened, the coffin was automatically pushed through them, and they closed again. The music and various metal grindings as the rollers rotated moving the coffin towards Marks oblivion, were the only sounds to be heard. He was dispatched.

We began to leave the building. I came face to face with the two men opposite. I thanked them for coming, informing them that I was Mark's landlady, and asking them how they had known him. One of them replied that they had previously worked with Mark, but that it had been many years ago. Both nodded. The second man added that they had not known Mark well. It seemed that nobody knew Mark well. The men offered no other comments. They looked alike. They both had very short crew cut hair styles and they wore long black surge coats. They were smart and clean cut. I had originally thought that they were part of the funeral director's entourage, but obviously not. They apologised for having to leave so abruptly, due to work commitments. They then turned and left quickly.

The chapel was still cold. We all left. I thanked the coroner for his concern and kindness to me during this awful period. I also thanked him for sending me a copy of the suicide letter. I drove Ann and me home. We chatted. She informed me that the woman, called Mona, who had recognised her was well known, almost a joke, in the local community. She was known as 'Mona the mourner', as she appeared to be a professional mourner. She liked to go to funerals and cremations. She would attend whether she knew the deceased or not. In fact, there had been many occasions when her presence had been resented. Many funerals were full. It would be difficult to find a seat. Her presence was not required. Ann told me that at one funeral, the deceased, who had been Mexican, had requested that a piñata be released. Close family had taken sticks to smash the piñata according to tradition. Mona, had pushed her way to the front insisting that she join in the action. The family had been affronted. We both laughed. I smiled as I reaffirmed that Ann certainly knew much about many people in the area. I wondered what information or pet sobriquet she would pass on about me? The assonance of 'Sonia, Suicides and Ashes Scattering a Speciality,' jumped into my head.

We arrived at Ann's house. I told her that I thought it would be good if we and the handyman, who often worked at the house and seemed to know Mark, could make a special visit to the local hill and scatter Mark's ashes, as he had wished. She agreed. I then offered to take us all out for a meal to celebrate Mark's life after we had scattered the ashes. She thought this too was a good idea. I said that perhaps Tom would like to join us, as he had also been involved in the drama. She said that he had only stayed one night with her. He had left the area, leaving his entire window cleaning paraphernalia at the house. Apparently he had been very annoyed because the police would not let him take it. He had been so annoyed that he told her that he would not stay in Cheltenham any longer. She said that she thought the whole experience had affected Tom more than he chose to show. Anyway, by now she was sure he would have replaced his ladders and got another job. He was a resourceful fellow and people always need window cleaners.

One week later the funeral director rang me, telling me that Mark's ashes would be ready for collection the following Wednesday. I contacted Ann and the handyman, telling them I would collect the ashes and then pick them both up from Ann's house at six o'clock. We would then continue to the hill so we could scatter the ashes. The informal ceremony would be followed by a meal in our local gastro-pub. The arrangements seemed suitable.

The next Wednesday soon came. It was a sunny hot day. A good day for scattering ashes. I drove to the undertakers with the car windows open wide, letting the excitable wind play with my acquiescent hair. I loved the wind. Twenty past five in the evening, saw me leaving the funeral parlour with a smart pink hessian bag containing a large box, in which I assumed were Mark's ashes. I suppose there is no way to check whose ashes are in the box. You just have to trust the undertakers. My thoughts wondered. If hospitals can swop newly born babies when they are discharged, how can undertakers know for certain whose ashes they are packaging? I carefully placed the bag, which I hoped contained Mark, on the passenger seat next to me. I could not put it in the boot. It was a person. It was Mark. I had to let his last journey be sitting next to me.

I had forgotten my purse. I needed to go home before going to Ann's. I soon reached my house and parked in the drive. I entered by the side gate. As soon as I opened the backdoor the phone began to ring. I rushed in and answered, but there was no one there. I listened for a bit, hoping someone would answer. No luck. I got my purse which I had left on the kitchen counter and returned to the car.

As I approached the car I realised something was wrong. I stood still, not believing what I was seeing. I stood still for some time. Not knowing what to do. Not knowing what to think. My open mouth gained acceptance before I did. It began to laugh. I always laugh when I am nervous. The passenger seat was empty. Mark, or whoever was in the box, had left the car. The bag had gone. Someone must have stolen it whilst I was in the house. My mouth continued laughing whilst my mind became totally confused. How would I explain this? Who had taken Mark? Why had they taken him? How could I lose him? I was responsible for him and now he had gone.

My mind computed; that's three goings in a few weeks. First, he had gone when I had found him in his bedsit. Second, he had gone when the coffin rolled him behind the curtains at the crematorium, and now he had gone from my car. Too many goings for my liking. What on earth was going on?

I stopped my nervous laughing. It was time to pick up Ann and the handyman. I got in the car and drove towards Ann's house. They were waiting outside. Soon we three were heading towards the hill.

I had to tell them what had happened. At first, I don't think they believed me, or they thought I was joking. Soon we were all laughing nervously. What do you do in a situation like that? Laughter seemed to help us process what had happened. By the time we reached the top of the hill, and the space where we had intended to scatter the ashes, our laughter had turned to concern and respect. We got out of the car. I offered a prayer. Ann said a few words saying she would miss him and the handyman added an apology for not bringing the ashes. We all looked glumly at each other. I then added that perhaps by now the thief had realised the mistake and would have returned the bag to my house. We drove from the hill expecting to find a pink hessian bag sitting by my front door. No such luck.

Despite our mixed emotions I thought it would be best to continue with our plans and eat. Food seems to ease most situations. Maybe after a meal we would return to find the bag sitting on my doorstep.

Two hours and three full stomachs later I returned home alone. No bag. Mark was well and truly gone. The third going. My religious childhood memories resounded in my brain. I had heard of a third coming. Jesus was supposed to have a third coming, but I had never heard of a third going.

I felt sad and emotional. I had not carried out Mark's wishes to the letter. I had let him down. I was not a person to be trusted. I slowly made my way indoors and to the hidden seclusion of my bed. I would hide. I would not have to face my failures until the morning. Sleep would help me process what had happened.

I awoke at eight on a bright sunny Thursday morning. I phoned my friend, Maureen. She had been a police officer for many years. She would know what to do. After telling her about my loss, she assured me that it was not my fault. She expected that the thief had thought the bag was mine and that there would be money or credit cards in it. Bag theft was rife. I felt slightly better. Well slightly better until she added that I must inform the coroner. Oh no, I would have to let that kind man know how inept I was. Isn't it strange but when you respect and like someone you so value their opinion, and you want them to respect and like you in return? My sobriquet changed to,

'Sonia, Suicides and Ashes Scattering a Speciality – Ashes Theft an Optional Extra.'

Nine o'clock found me on the phone apologising to my delightful coroner. He seemed to take it all in his stride. He did not blame me. In fact, he suggested that he completely understood how this could have happened and that I was not to concern myself over the loss. I was just to leave everything to him. He would inform the police, hoping that the bag may have been handed in to them. It would all be alright. I was not to give it another thought.

I returned to my planned activities for the day. Too much had been happening since Mark's suicide. I wanted my life to return to its usual unexciting normality.

This it did. Well, this it did for about four weeks. Four weeks after the dilemma with the ashes, two strangers rang my doorbell. I was not sure how I was feeling. I had previously learnt that a friend had died. I was in that strange state of non-feeling. Not knowing where my emotions should be found or what I should be feeling. Not wanting to be too upset, as she was not a very close friend, but wanting to be sad enough to be respectfully affected.

I remembered when my father had died. Eventually when the shock had left me, and I was alone, I cried and cried. I cried so much and yet I was so annoyed with myself. These tears I shed for my beloved father seemed to be the same tears I would shed whilst watching a sad movie or listening to sorrowful music. I wanted better tears. I wanted my father to know my tears were of the best quality. They were the best tears I could offer. I cry now as I remember this. I try to save my best emotions for my worst situations. My logical self thinks perhaps this is a good way to manage life. Surely when we are at our worst or in our worst situations, it is then that we need to muster our best abilities and our best emotions. Perhaps the worst things that happen to us can allow us to offer our best selves? Our best selves help us to continue living, hopefully living well. I wondered how many refugees or victims of trauma manage to find their best selves? I think if I were in their position, I am not sure I would be able to find my best self. I only hope that my father has forgiven me for shedding typical rather than special tears.

The doorbell rang again. I opened the front door. A man and a woman stood looking at me.

'So sorry to disturb you but are you Mark Mobley's land-lady?' asked the man.

My immediate affirmation allowed him to continue.

'We are his friends. We would like to talk to you about what happened to him.'

I was still feeling emotional regarding the loss of my friend. I felt so sorry for the two of them.

'Please come in,' was my empathetic reply. 'I am so sorry for your loss,' I politely added.

I showed them both into the lounge. They introduced themselves. He as David and she as Janet. I told them to feel free to call me Sonia. (I did not mention my imagined soubriquet.) We sat and they asked me again what had happened to Mark. I was not sure how much I should disclose. How much would Mark want me to share with these two? I turned their questions round.

'Well, what do you know already?' I asked.

They informed me that they had seen the notices in the local paper and that they had contacted the coroner. He had informed them of the suicide and cremation. Sadly, they had been unable to attend the cremation due to Covid restrictions.

I told them there was little I could add. I explained that although Mark had lived in one of my bedsits, I hardly knew him. I felt so sorry for their loss. I offered tea. They accepted. I left them sitting in the lounge whilst I made the tea. We drank and made polite conversation. I told them that I had needed to have Mark's room cleared, but that I had kept his watch and glasses, just in case he had a friend or relative who would have wanted to receive something of his. There had also been a strange necklace made of a black bead on a ribbon which I had also kept. I wanted something of Mark's for myself. I kept the strange necklace in the top drawer of my desk. I showed them the watch and glasses, which I had placed in a transparent plastic freezer bag along with his suicide note. They asked to see the copy of the suicide note. I gave it to them. It recalled an emotional time for me. I did not want to read it again. I let them read it silently whilst I finished my tea. They thanked me and said they did not want the watch or glasses. I had not shown them the necklace. For some reason I wanted to keep it. It seemed strange but at the same time I knew it must have been precious to Mark. I did not want to let it go. They stood to leave.

As they left the lounge and entered the hall, I had a brainwave. I had a student's A4 notepad and a pencil on my hall table.

'Please leave me your name and address. If I think of anything else, I will be able to get in touch with you.'

They smiled, obviously thinking this was a good idea. The man took the pad and wrote his name and address in large print. I watched him do it. He then placed the pad back on the hall table. The woman began looking at the knick-knacks in my hall cabinet. She said she like the musical boxes and the small jugs. I took out one of my favourite music boxes. I wound it up and we both listened as it tinkled Beethoven's 'Für Elise'. We laughed as we discussed the contrast between the richness of Beethoven's masterpiece and the crude tinny noise of the musical box. We chatted a bit, and they both left.

I returned to the kitchen and my cooking. My sister would be arriving for the weekend, and I needed to prepare food. The end of an evening of cooking saw me heading upstairs to bed. I was tired.

My sister arrived the next morning. We sat in the kitchen and had our usual elevenses, coffee and biscuits. I was telling her about the visitors of the day before. I had already told her on the phone about the Mark scenario of the previous weeks. She listened attentively. I went into the hall to get the A4 pad to show her the names of Mark's friends. The pad was there but the page on which the man had written had been ripped off. I looked askance. Who had done this and why? Had someone come into the house whilst I was asleep? Stop, I was getting paranoid. No one could have entered my house. No one else had been in the hall. It could only have been Mark's friends themselves.

I put the pad on the kitchen bar and went into the lounge. The dirty teacups were still on the tray. I looked around. The file had gone. Mark's suicide note, his glasses, his watch, everything belonging to Mark had disappeared. I computed that they could only have been taken by his so-called 'friends'. I was at a loss as to what to think. I had offered them the things. Why had they stolen them? Why had they removed their contact details? What was happening? I began to feel uneasy about the situation. I was glad my sister was with me. She could offer me support. I suddenly felt very shivery and strange. I didn't know why. Why should I feel strange? I had done nothing, except perhaps lose Mark's ashes. But really, I had done nothing and now I was feeling very upset and even apprehensive. I did not understand. Both my sister and I returned to drinking our coffees and now eating too many comforting chocolate biscuits. The only thing I had to remind me of Mark was the black necklace in my desk drawer. We continued eating the biscuits.

The penetrating sound of the doorbell interrupted our food fest. I was relieved to find my friend Maureen standing in front of me.

'What's the matter,' she asked. 'You look as if you've seen the proverbial ghost!'

She came in and joined my sister and me in the kitchen. I made more coffee and put out more biscuits. I explained exactly what had happened the evening before with Mark's friends. Both my sister and Maureen listened without interruption.

When I had finished, Maureen put her arm around me and told me not to worry. She affirmed that I now had nothing at all belonging to Mark. Mark and anything he owned had been totally removed from my life. There was no sign that he had ever existed. Yet again he had gone. I did not mention the necklace.

Maureen wanted to know what I had told his friends. I told her what I had repeated to everyone since his death; that is, that I knew very little about him. Very little at all. He was a very private individual. I did not know him well.

She said that my ignorance was most probably the saving of me. She connected the two men at the crematorium and the two friends of the previous evening. She felt both sets were somehow involved in Mark's work, either with the American Intelligence Agency or with the British Government Intelligence Agency. She thought that Mark's secrecy was part of his job, but also a way of protecting me. She felt his work colleagues were trying to be assured that I knew nothing of his work or of anything he was involved in. Maureen took the notepad and ran the pencil over the indentations, hoping to reveal the information which the man had previously written. I remembered doing just such an activity when I had played 'spies and James Bond' games in my childhood. Policing had obviously not improved much. Nothing showed up on the paper.

I voiced my disbelief out loud as I said,

'I still can't understand why they stole the things. I had offered them the glasses, and the watch. Why would they just steal them?'

Maureen replied that now I would not be able to confirm whether or not they actually had the items. All I could say was that I did not know where the items were. I could only surmise that they had been stolen, but I could not say with any conviction or proof who had stolen them.

I was beginning to see a sinister side to the past few weeks. I accepted Maureen's appraisal of the situation. She was right in saying that perhaps my ignorance had really protected me. I wanted to extricate myself from any future involvement with anything to do with Mark. I would tell my friendly coroner of the visit of Mark's so-called 'friends', and about Mark's possessions being stolen and then that would be it. I would no longer be involved. I was only his landlady. I did not want anything more to do with the situation.

Suddenly I remembered the letter I had secreted in my pocket on the day of the suicide. I had forgotten all about it. I must have been so involved with everything going on that I had dismissed it. I had not looked at it. Things had been too busy and emotional. Gosh, the scarecrows would really think that I was concealing evidence again. I decided to just ignore it. I did not want to know. Since Mark had died, my life had been turned upside down. Now I was beginning to feel frightened. Something was amiss but I did not know what. I was beginning to be afraid. My head sent an electric current down my spine. I shivered again.

Maureen, trying to cheer me up, jokingly suggested that I should not touch any door knobs. At first I did not understand what she was talking about, then I remembered the people in Salisbury who had been poisoned, supposedly by the foreign Secret Service agents. Mark had visited many different countries, perhaps agents were after him? Her joke fell on deaf ears. I did not find it funny.

I was scared, not knowing what might happen next. Everything was becoming too strange. Mark had left me, yet I knew I would never forget him or the drama he had released into my life. I ate yet another chocolate biscuit.

CHAPTER FIVE

JO JOINS GOVERNMENT INTELLIGENCE AGENCY – TEN YEARS BEFORE COVID

'There are no norms. All people are exceptions to a rule that does not exist.'

Fernando Pessoa, *The Book of Disquiet*

He was exceptionally exceptional! Jo had arrived at the Government Intelligence Agency amid a tsunami of gossip. His reputation had preceded him. He could speak nine languages fluently. At the age of fifteen he had won a Mastermind trophy after answering questions on European Palaces. He had been given unlimited access to numerous historical sites and buildings for research purposes and he had been a successful male model. His educational trajectory had been just as exceptional. He had achieved his first degree in mathematics at the age of sixteen, followed by a masters at eighteen, which he subsequently transmuted into a doctorate.

He had joined the intelligence arm of the army and been deployed to many foreign parts. He had quickly been given special assignments. Due to his language skills and obvious intelligence, he had been head-hunted and joined the Government Intelligence Agency when he was twenty seven. For one so young he seemed to have fulfilled many demanding accomplishments. He soon became known as the 'Golden Boy'.

Despite all his achievements, the one frivolous area in which he excelled seemed to be his personal flare and delight in fashion. He would wear all sorts of colours and fabrics and he enjoyed wearing make-up. At one time he even arrived for work in a skirt. He was beautiful to look at, with shoulder length, dark blond hair, striking blue eyes, fair skin and long limbs. His six-foot six-inch frame always moved gracefully. To look at he was a tall, sort of pre-Covid Olly Alexander, but with long hair. However, some of the older members of the establishment were suspicious of his looks and flamboyant attire, which transgressed their understanding of what was acceptable in such a distinguished workplace as the Government Intelligence Agency.

Many of the women would try to talk to him when he arrived or left work. They would offer to bring him coffee when he insisted remaining at his workstation. Despite all their best efforts to get close to him, he remained aloof. He made no friends. He kept himself to himself whilst numerous colleagues, of both sexes, were fascinated by his unconventional looks and intriguing personality. They would try to engage him in conversation or share a tea break with him. He tactfully evaded each approach. He appeared to be a social isolate. The buzz going around was that he was gender fluid or that he had some sort of personality disorder, though I don't think anyone really understood about either issue. It was all just idle gossip. Idle gossip that can do irreparable harm. People just seemed to have needed a label in order to help them understand why he appeared so different.

The only member of staff who seemed to be able to engage him in any type of conversation was his direct line manager. The two men were forced to work together, focusing on their forays into 'listening to incomprehensible conversations' from numerous far-flung countries around the world or decoding obscure messages. They both spoke Russian fluently and would often converse in that language to ensure that those around them could not understand what was being said. The two men would work together most days. Jo always appeared to be able to untangle many, seemingly incomprehensible, communications which were being picked up. The respect between the two men grew steadily.

Jo was neither happy nor sad working at the Government Intelligence Agency. It was just another job to him. Another way of earning money and spending his time. Though the pay was not as good as he had expected, he found the privacy and secrecy surrounding the place to be useful for him. He felt comfortable, as long as he could be working alone or with just one other person. Limiting his social interactions meant that he would be able to manage. He did not want to be around people. He did not want to have to make conversation. He hated conversation. He would not show it, but inside he felt overwhelmed by the proximity of people. He had always tried to hide and just disappear in many group situations.

He thought he knew how to manage his world. Hiding was his first instinct. But often it hadn't worked. People would not leave him alone. If he was viewed as the quiet or unapproachable individual in the workplace, his colleagues would feel sorry for him and try to include him in such activities as sharing lunch, going on pub visits, or even just having a cup of tea. They would not let him be left alone. People were forever targeting him for a multiplicity of reasons.

In order to ensure that those kind individuals who would insist on trying to include him in their social whirl were deployed elsewhere, he had devised a new strategy. He employed this new strategy soon after he began his work at the Government Intelligence Agency. He would look as striking and colourful as possible. He would appear confident and aloof. He would adopt the persona of a totally fulfilled and accomplished, self-actualising superman. This deception would ensure that people would not be able to feel sorry for him. They would not try to include him in their activities. They would feel overawed by his good looks and imposing demeanour. He could, by being totally over the top, keep people away from him. Thus far it seemed to have worked. Most people, men and women alike, kept their distance from him. Now he felt they were automatically just ignoring him. He was something they could not quite understand. He was not like them. He was different.

This new strategy was put into effect a few weeks after Jo entered the Government Intelligence Agency. He was wearing a pale eau-de-nil silk shirt, with dark emerald green twill chinos and a white cashmere scarf. Emerald green was Jo's favourite colour. On his feet he wore a pair of his favourite designer white suede loafers, which had cost a fortune. He always felt confident in his loafers, owning six pairs in various colours. He ensured that he looked amazing, maintaining an aloof confidence in preparation to face whatever the Government Intelligence Agency would throw at him.

Since his arrival, Jo was fortunate to have been placed under the guidance of a lead analyst called Mark Mobley. Mark was a man of few words. It was strange that although Mark and Jo were fluent in many languages, they found communication with fellow humans as both problematic and unnecessary. Their similar predispositions towards quiet and contemplative existences allowed a perfect balance to be established in their relationship. They would sit side by side for hours … just listening … listening to feeds coming from all sorts of devices and numerous different sources … feeds from all over the globe. Although they both understood many different languages, their skills were even more developed than just being interpretive. They could also recognise a range of different accents and inflections or emphases, giving them clues as to the general geographical whereabouts of the transmissions. They were talented and exacting. They were insightful and discriminating. But their skills were for their work, not for any interpersonal agendas. They were social recluses. They neither needed nor wanted to communicate or interact with those around them. Their screens were their companions.

Soon Jo had become the right-hand man for Mark. They seemed inseparable. Their work was always of a high standard, and they were well respected and admired by their colleagues. All their communications were verbal. They never exchanged looks or expressions. They were never seen laughing or chatting together. They appeared almost void of human characteristics. They were quite robotic in their shared work world. Nevertheless, this sterile way of communicating seemed to serve them well. They both found solace in emotional silence and introspective aloneness.

On a particularly bright Monday morning, Mark took up his position next to Jo in front of the plethora of screens, speakers and relay monitors. Jo had already started work. He ignored Mark's arrival and just carried on with his usual activities. Mark, tapped him on the shoulder to get his attention, saying quietly,

'We have been chosen to do some work for the American Intelligence Agency. We will leave on Wednesday.'

Jo showed no emotion, he just nodded and returned to his work. Mark was slightly taken aback. He would have expected at least some questions. The sort of questions he would have asked. Indeed, the sort of questions he had already asked. For instance,

'How long? Where to? What will we be doing?'

Jo did not seem to need any of these insights. Jo appeared devoid of curiosity.

Mark put his thoughts regarding Jo's lack of interest to the back of his mind, and carried on listening to some interesting Russian conversations which were coming out of Crimea. The rest of the week continued without event.

However, the following Wednesday saw both Mark and Jo, being driven to Heathrow airport with cases, passports and visas. Mark smiled to himself as he realised that Jo still had no idea where they were going, what they were expected to do, or for what purpose? Jo seemed to have no curiosity at all. They negotiated passport and security checks with ease. Their papers were obviously not only in order but also super effective. Super effective in diminishing the egocentric power trips festering in many uniformed airport officials. They were escorted quickly and respectfully through each security challenge. They were soon settled in their first-class seats on a flight to Daniel K. Inouye International Airport, located in Honolulu on the island of Oahu. There would be one change of plane on the trip, which would entail a two-hour stopover in Los Angeles. Mark did not see this as problematic as the first-class seats and service ensured that they would be comfortable most of the time. They were both avid readers and had prepared for the trip by each placing three novels in their hand luggage.

Mark had visited Hawaii some years before. He had found the islands alluring. As a teenager he had seen an Elvis Presley movie called *Blue Hawaii* and enjoyed the vistas and seascapes of the magical islands. He began to hum the tune 'Blue Hawaii' in his head. Elvis had told him that dreams might come true in Blue Hawaii. Mark did not believe in dreams, nevertheless he still wondered if perhaps his would one day become true.

He was looking forward to the trip. Even when Jo realised their destination, he still seemed unfazed by the idea of visiting such beautiful islands. Mark wondered what would affect Jo. Nothing, except work, seemed to interest him. Perhaps if he had seen Elvis in the film, he would have considered the islands to hold some sort of magic for him. Mark looked at Jo's vacant face. Jo showed no expression, no feeling, no emotion. Just beautiful vacant stillness, almost like a Michelangelo statue.

Mark was Jo's line manager. He considered the last staff appraisal he had carried out. He had given Jo much feedback as he evaluated his performance. He considered areas for improvement and development, and discussed avenues that could lead to promotion, but at all times Jo had shown no emotional response. No response to neither good nor bad feedback. No response at all. This had forced Mark's hand. He decided to mention an area which he knew was challenging for Jo. He asked Jo about his commitment to 'team building' and his views on the importance of working with groups and colleagues. Again, Jo showed no emotional reaction. He just stated in a matter-of-fact way,

'Well of course, both you and I know that we share the same views on these issues. We are perfectly in sync.'

Mark realised that Jo was correct. Neither of them needed nor wanted to take part in any team building, nor did they want the inclusion of developing interpersonal skills to be part of their job descriptions. They were both loners.

Mark settled into the comfort of the first-class seats. Hawaii called …

After many hours, much reading, sleeping and one change of plane they arrived at their destination. They 'deplaned' as the American air hostess had instructed and were hit by an envelope of hot humid air and vast blue skies. A group of five smiling women approached them, putting rainbow-coloured leis around their necks and mouthing sweet alohas. Mark felt his lei. It was made of some sort of stiff fabric. It would last forever. He felt 'ersatz' as he remembered the fresh moist sweet-smelling flowered lei he had received on his previous visit.

He knew he would find changes. The YumYum Tree, where he had eaten steak and eggs had gone out of business. He had never seen Honolulu's iconic Woolworths, though locals still talked about it with remembered affection. His mind reached out to the last time he had enjoyed surfing and snorkeling at Diamond Head and been overwhelmed by the range and colours of the marine life.

'Stop,' he told himself. 'Stop thinking about the past. It is the present that matters. You are here to work not to enjoy yourself. Just focus on the moment.'

His forays into the importance of practising mindfulness leapt to the front of his consciousness.

Mark had been undergoing therapy for some years, though he had not told anyone at work. He found life difficult. He found people difficult. His inner world belonged to shades of murky browns and greys. He looked around. The hues of Hawaii were a vibrant, almost painful contrast to his shadowing sensibilities. He forced his mind to consider the work they were about to begin. He could usually cope if he put his mind into work mode.

It was as if the universe smiled on him. The universe knew what he needed. Just as Cinderella had been sent her Fairy Godmother to rescue her from the drudgery of her painful existence, a Fairy Godfather had been placed at the arrivals gate, ready to take over Mark's life and transport him to his preferred world. Mark could hear music coming from the speakers around the airport. It was one of his favourites, Lady Gaga singing, 'Born This Way'. Mark knew what way he had been born.

The Fairy Godfather shook Mark's hand as he introduced himself. He was a senior member of the American Intelligence Agency, dressed in faded jeans and a dowdy shirt. Mark had met him on his previous visit. He knew that despite his casual appearance this man was a sharp and insightful individual. After shaking hands, they walked towards the exit. Mark's Fairy Godfather would save him from the terrors of tempting tourism and transport him into a world where he felt comfortable and where he belonged ... the 'World of Work'.

The three men left the airport in a chauffeur driven car and were soon transported to the tourist free part of the island away from the crowded hedonistic beaches which enticed most new arrivals.

It was late on a Saturday evening when Mark and Jo were eventually ensconced in their respective billets and given files containing all the information they would need for the next few days. The secure compound where they were to stay was extensive. It was surrounded by secure fencing and numerous tall lights. However, most of the work was carried out underground.

Mark's Fairy Godfather had left, but before he left, he had told both men that they would not start work until Monday at eight a.m. However, they needed to be ready at nine a.m. the following morning because a car was being sent for them. They were to experience a day of Hawaiian hospitality at the expense of the American Intelligence Agency! Mark had never heard of such a thing. The American Intelligence Agency rarely 'gave' anything, let alone a day of hospitality. However, he knew not to argue. So, despite having many reservations, he had just thanked his Fairy Godfather and turned his attentions to unpacking his small suitcase. He logically realised that the Sunday of hospitality would allow recovery from the long journey and the debilitations of the dreaded 'jetlag'.

Mark finished putting his few clothes into the closet then left his room to check on Jo. Jo had a similar suite of rooms across the corridor. They made cursory comments about the accommodation and the imminent day of enforced hospitality programmed for the next morning. Then Mark suggested that they both ate the food which had been left on trays in their rooms and went straight to bed. He handed Jo two paracetamols, telling him that they might help any jet lag symptoms and maybe enhance his sleep. He then returned to his room, had a shower, ate the food which had been left on the table and got into bed. Sleep soon came.

He awoke the next morning at seven with a headache, slouched his way into the bathroom, and then explored the small kitchenette.

'Yes,' he considered the various offerings which had been left. Coffee, fruit and cornflakes would help him begin the day. He then remembered the threat of the forthcoming 'Day of American Intelligence Agency Hospitality'.

'Oh no,' his antisocial predisposition yelled within his head.

'Oh NO!' it loudly echoed.

Despite his reservations regarding the day ahead, Mark had many fond memories of Hawaii. Many years earlier, when he had first starting working for the Government Intelligence Agency, he had been sent to work there for a month. This first visit had interrupted the weekly counselling sessions he was undertaking. He was concerned that he would not be able to cope. However, he was still able to talk to his counsellor on the phone, so he managed to negotiate the situation well.

Although he had not had much time for enjoying touristy activities, he did find time to surf. He replayed the song 'Cool Down' by Kolohe Kai in his head. Its lyrics reminded him that the time he had spent in Hawaii had been filled with the love and fellowship of Aloha and pride.

Life had seemed much easier then. He was able to do as all Hawaiians tried to do and just 'hang loose'. On his first and only previous trip he had also bought a couple of Aloha shirts, which he had packed in his suitcase for this return trip. One was quite acceptable, being a profusion of large emerald green palm leaves scattered across a white cotton background. The second was more extravagant, showing pink flamingos and orange flowers on a baby blue background. He wondered why he had ever bought them. They were completely out of character. After showering he put on the green and white shirt, taking the other across the corridor to Jo. Jo opened the door and accepted the shirt Mark was holding out towards him. Then he noted the shirt Mark was wearing.

'But I prefer that shirt, emerald green is my favourite colour. I want that shirt!'

'But I am already wearing it,' was Mark's forced reply.

To this Jo offered a curt, 'thank you' and closed the door. Mark returned to his room to await their hour of departure, nine a.m.

Ten minutes past nine, on a bright sunny Sunday morning saw both men, dressed as tourists, sitting in the back of a white Mercedes heading for one of the island's many beaches. Jo looked resplendent in Mark's colourful flamingo shirt, pink shorts, gold flip flops and the rainbow lei of the day before. Mark wore khaki shorts, the green and white shirt and sensible brown leather sandals. They both wore dark glasses, to hide their respective characters and their shared unease.

The particular beach they were being taken to was one which held traditional luaus on the last Sunday of every month. A luau is a Hawaiian party which is held on a beach and is usually an excuse for often hundreds of people to get together and celebrate. Most Hawaiians would be happy to celebrate anything, from losing a tooth to recovering from a major disease ... anything.

Party is probably too limiting a word. A luau can last all day and all evening. Indeed, some have even lasted all night too. On arrival a whole pig is wrapped in palm leaves and placed in a large pit dug in the sand. The pig is buried in the pit, which is then surrounded by burning embers. The smouldering pig within its green sarcophagus is almost forgotten for the rest of the day; only to be removed from its hot bed of ashes in the early evening; having been slow cooked to perfection and ready to become part of the pulled pork experience of the hungry party goers.

Daytime luau activities can include many games and quasi sport challenges both on land and in the water. Dancing and music would enhance all the organised games whilst everything would be lubricated by various cocktails and soft drinks. Towards early evening and before the pig could be served, there would be a group fishing event. Long nets would have previously been caste early in the morning. Before the evening meal, men and women would enter the sea and retrieve the crescent of netting, moving the net towards an imaginary centre point, thus catching all the fish enclosed within the netted circle. Dependent upon the number of fish being caught, loud yelps of joy and cheers of achievement would ripple through the air. Skilled cooks would fillet and grill the fish on several barbecues.

Excitement, fun and camaraderie were the watchwords which supported every luau. The whole experience sought to be escapist and entertaining. Sadly, for both Mark and Jo, the whole experience would be overwhelming, causing them both much discomfort and distress. The only escapism they would find acceptable would be to escape from the noise, movement, people and activity associated with any luau. Both men were saturated with anxiety.

They were both bright. They knew they would have to find a way to cope with this day of enforced frivolity and fun. Without speaking, indeed without even looks of understanding, they both moved away from the pit where the unfortunate pig was being prepared. They moved towards a glade of trees at the top of the beach, behind what must have been the 'toilets block'. They could stay within the green glade. No one would be able to see them, and they were more than content to forgo any partying. They scooped hollows into the soft sand and sat in relative comfort. Jo looked at Mark saying,

'I feel like Peter Pan, hiding away from Captain Hook. You can be a Lost Boy if you like.'

With that he threw a few sprinkles of sand onto Mark's lap saying,

'This is pixie dust and we can now fly away to Never Never Land in a cloud of green wonder.'

Mark explained to Jo that there really were beaches in Hawaii that had green sand. He had visited Diamond Head where Olivine deposits or 'Hawaiian Diamond' could be found. The Olivine would turn the sand a green shade. Jo looked interested. Mark was amazed as there were few things that did interested Jo.

'Can we go to Diamond Head? Green is my favourite colour,' Jo asked.

'No time,' was Mark's curt reply.

They then took out their phones and the murder mystery books they had secreted in their pockets, in readiness for their own self chosen solitary enjoyments. The trees and some small bushes meant that they were fairly well hidden from those they did not wish to meet. Indeed, though not in Never Never Land they were in a sort of green glade. Apart from leaving their self-designed sanctuary in order to get food or liquid, they did not need to join the Hawaiian hospitality so generously offered to them. They remained in the glade for most of the day. Fortunately, Captain Hook did not come near them. They were protected by the verdant shrubbery which surrounded them.

The only thing which disturbed their peace was when two young women began to move towards the trees. One of the women was crying. The other was trying to comfort her. Could it be Tinker Bell and her friend had entered the drama?

'Look at me,' the distressed Tinker Bell sobbed.

She opened her mouth to reveal two large front teeth, which were a strange shade of bright blue. She explained to the woman comforting her that the curacao in the numerous 'Blue Hawaii' cocktails she had been drinking had stained the new implants she had just had fitted in readiness for her wedding photos.

'What will Elmer do?' she whined. 'It's the first day of our honeymoon and his new wife has blue teeth!'

The stained wife, recently renamed Tinker Bell by our Peter Pan and his Lost Boy, continued with her sobbing as she and her comforter left the glade and headed back towards the party. Both Mark and Jo returned to their phone activities without comment. They neither wondered nor cared what 'Elmer' would do. Jo had been slightly confused by the whole affair. The only Elmer he knew was a brightly coloured patchwork elephant he had possessed during his childhood. Anyway, he thought that like him, the elephant wouldn't care what colour the sobbing woman's teeth were. He returned his attention to the games on his phone. Tinker Bell and her comforter were soon forgotten.

The day progressed without further incident. Tinker Bell had vanished; Captain Hook had never appeared; so Peter and the Lost Boy had been left alone to their own devices.

The taxi arrived for them at the pre-arranged time of nine p.m. and they were returned to their billets. Aching and exhausted after spending much of the day in their individual sand holes, they were both eager to shower and get into bed.

Their week in Hawaii had begun badly. Things could only improve.

Indeed, things did improve. Work, work and more work seemed to offer just what they both needed. The only other trip they made during their time on the island, was to the Pearl Habor National Memorial Park. Mark hoped that DNA and new scientific technologies would allow the bodies of service men and women lost on the *USS Arizona* on 7 December 1941, to be finally returned to their families for burial. They both seemed to enjoy the visit.

They had much work to do together. It seemed that most of their American colleagues would expect them to work on their various projects in tandem. Despite usually working alone, even when sitting side by side, it seemed they were now having to negotiate working co-operatively. At first neither of them felt comfortable, but as the week progressed, they began to feel less stressed with the enforced work pattern.

Jo remembered the problems he had had as an infant. His teacher had discussed his inability to play with other children. He had heard her explaining to his mum that usually children would move on from playing alongside others, what she called parallel play, to working together and co-operating with each other. The teacher felt concerned about Jo's social and emotional development. Jo, it appeared wanted to stay at the solitary play stage. His mum did not seem concerned. She knew he was bright. She told the teacher that he would be alright as he had a good mind. His mum was right. But now here he was in Hawaii and having to practise a sort of co-operative play, or rather work, with Mark. He knew he was bright. He heard his mum's words again and he knew he would be alright. He was managing well. The time passed quickly. They worked every day, even weekends until eventually the time came to think about returning to Gloucestershire and the Government Intelligence Agency.

It was the evening before they were to leave and head for England. Their Fairy Godfather had insisted on taking them for a meal at a popular Japanese restaurant on Waikiki beach. Jo hoped, unrealistically, that he might see Komodo Dragons or wandering peacocks. His romantic impression of Waikiki beach was destroyed by Mark, who suggested that the only things they would find on the beach would be discarded syringes or used condoms.

They both felt obliged to accept their Fairy Godfather's invitation, though they would have preferred just to eat together. They had begun to feel comfortable in each other's company. They each had different reasons for wanting to spend their last evening alone together, without any other company.

Jo's reason was straightforward. Jo never wanted nor sought company. Jo preferred his solitary existence to remain solitary. He could accept Mark because Mark seemed to understand him. Mark would not be intrusive. Mark demanded nothing from him. Mark just let him be.

However, Mark's reason for spending their last evening together came from a completely different place. Mark felt he had been getting closer to Jo with every day since their initial meeting. On first encountering Jo he had been overwhelmed. It was not just Jo's obvious beauty, or his intellectual capacity, or even his many accomplishments. It was the two dimples in his cheeks. The dimples were hardly visible. Jo rarely showed expressions but when he felt happy small dimples would begin to appear. Mark knew and understood the reasons for these dimples. Mark understood Jo. Mark knew the problems of being challenged by so called mental disorders. Mark admired Jo; indeed, he eventually began to like him. But before even liking could begin in a rational way, Mark had been engulfed in an overwhelming limerence when Jo first arrived at the Government Intelligence Agency. A limerence which had, during the many hours they had spent together, developed and crystallised into what he now felt as 'pure love'.

Mark had known about limerence for some time. He realised that it could be seen as a negative state, a way of wanting another to fulfil you, whether they were good for you or not. It could be seen as wanting to be saved by another. At the same time, you would ignore any flaws and see the object of your limerence as 'perfect'. He had felt limerence before. He knew its pitfalls. His therapy had alerted him to the damage of such unrealistic thoughts. Thoughts he had often harboured towards many unsuspecting younger men. He had at last come to terms with his homosexuality. He could not ignore it. He had also begun to understand his frequent feelings of limerence. But it took this trip to Hawaii and being with Jo most of the time, to assure him that he was at last, truly in love. He convinced himself that his feelings were now pure love. What he felt for Jo was not limerence. He felt his feelings were reciprocated. He felt that they needed each other. He knew Jo was just holding back because of shyness. He knew Jo wanted to be with him as much as he wanted to be with Jo. Limerence had been replaced by love. He was experiencing pure love for his very own 'golden boy' who so readily earned such a label. Peter Pan and the Lost Boy were destined to be together. Mark was sure of it.

The evening arrived for their special dinner. The Fairy Godfather sent a car for them at six pm. The timing would allow them to watch the sunset over the sea. They were soon walking on Waikiki beach. The popular Japanese restaurant was packed. A concoction of different nationalities, shapes, genders, and sizes surrounded the building, some of which attempted to form a disorderly queue. Their Fairy God-father emerged from the mass and welcomed them both, indicating for them to follow him. They passed the foray of hopefuls waiting to be given tables and moved towards the middle of the restaurant.

The centre of the restaurant held a large domed area. Under the dome the space was taken up by an enormous hot plate, approximately one by two metres in size. A rim of wooden 'table' enclosed three sides of the hot plate. Eight chairs had been placed around this rim. Four in front and two at each side. The Fairy Godfather directed Mark and Jo to sit either side of him at the front. Others then filled up the remaining five seats. Both Mark and Jo felt acute dis-comfort and anxiety when the unknown individuals joined their party. Apparently, sitting with unknown individuals was the norm in some popular Hawaiian restaurants. Space was at a premium and shared space was usual.

The Japanese chef stood opposite them. There was no wooden rim between him and the hot plate. The hot plate was to become the chef's palate. He would remain standing at the plate and cook whatever the diners required. They would place their orders and the raw food would arrive ready to be cooked. In order to maintain a fun element at this very popular restaurant, each chef, for there were twelve hot plates strategically placed around the interior and each hot plate was attended by a chef, each chef would try to outdo the others. They would throw utensils, salt and pep-per pots, food, bottles, all sorts, into the air like jugglers.

They would dance whilst cooking and disperse the cooked food by throwing it onto plates which had been strategically placed in front of each diner sitting at the wooded surround. It was all very dramatic and impressive. Most people found it an engaging and fun way to share a meal.

Sadly, both Mark and Jo would have wished to have been anywhere else on the planet rather than sharing this eating space with strangers. At last, the meal was over. They were both pleased to have come to the end of their evening with the Fairy Godfather. After a couple of forced 'thank you for a wonderful evening' our reluctant diners left their seats and approached their waiting taxi, ready to be returned to their billets.

They were soon driving into the secure area at the base where they had been stationed. On entering the building, Mark suggested that he and Jo should share a last drink together to celebrate the completion of their work in Hawaii and the end of an awful evening.

Mark wanted some quiet time with Jo. He had bought Jo a special gift. It was a black Kukui nut necklace threaded onto a thin black grosgrain ribbon. He knew that in Hawaii, the Kukui nut symbolised the energy of love and peace. The Kukui tree represented enlightenment, offering a link between this world and the next. Mark had bought two identical necklaces. One for him and one for Jo.

He knew that he and Jo were twin souls. They shared a similar vibration in this world. They understood each other. They had similar likes and dislikes. They were meant to be together.

They both entered Mark's room. Mark opened two cans of Dole pineapple juice. He turned to Jo and gave him the juice, and then he passed him a pink paper bag. Jo put the can down and pulled the necklace from its bag.

'Oh, it is beautiful, and so Hawaiian. I adore it. I will so enjoy wearing it. Thank you so much.'

Mark had never heard Jo be so enthusiastic about anything. He noticed Jo's dimples appear. How he loved those dimples. He realised that everything was going to plan.

'Help me put it on,' Jo pleaded, handing Mark the necklace and turning his back to him.

Mark gently placed the necklace around Jo's neck and secured it. Jo raised his hand placing it on the shiny black nut. He turned to show Mark. At that moment Mark leaned forward and kissed him. The two men froze. They looked into each other's eyes. Mark, realising he had misread the situation, quickly tried to recoup his position,

'But, I love you. I have loved you since the first time I set eyes on you.'

He paused, waiting for a response. Nothing came. Jo just looked bewildered. Mark tried again.

'You must know that I love you. Haven't I shown you in so many ways? I understand you. I am always thinking of you. Do you not love me? Do you not love me even a little?'

Mark realised that yet again in his life he had misread other's feelings. Perhaps his decision that limerence had been replaced by love was another mistake. Mark began to question all his assumptions. He had been sure that Jo felt what he was feeling. He had been sure that they were in love. He shivered as he began to feel confused and lost. His world was starting to feel unreal. His body felt as if it were disintegrating around him.

Jo did not move. He closed his eyes, then opened them again. As Mark wondered what to do next, Jo just turned, and still wearing his enlightenment necklace left the room and closed the door quietly behind him. He had heard the last words that were ever to be spoken between them.

CHAPTER SIX

DANGLING DEPRESSION AND
JO'S DEPARTURE – BEFORE COVID

'To live is to be other. Even feeling is impossible if one feels today what one felt yesterday for that is not to feel. It is only to remember today what one felt yesterday, to be living in the corpse of yesterday's lost life.'

Fernando Pessoa, *The Book of Disquiet*

Both Mark and Jo wished their yesterdays had not existed, or if they had to exist that they would become crystallised within the corpses of their lost lives, soon to be forgotten.

Their time in Hawaii had ended abruptly. The return trip to England was demanding to say the least. Not just because of the distance, or the change of planes, or even the confined space on the planes. It was demanding because both Mark and Jo were experiencing heightened anxiety and fear. They did not speak; they did not look at each other. Two strained strangers sitting side by side, were independently circumnavigating half the globe and returning to the Government Intelligence Agency.

From his late teens Mark had suffered from bouts of what he called dangling depression. He knew only too well of the demands of coping with lost periods of lethargy, vacancy and searing pain. He knew that even if he were able to offer some semblance of normality to keep his parents happy, that eventually his fears would find him again and return him to his lost state. He felt that the most debilitating thing about his particular experience of being depressed was that it was so unpredictable. He never knew why or when it would engulf him. Consequently, he never really trusted himself.

All those around him would plan their lives, consider their activities and prepare schedules to help them through each day. He would never want to plan anything, just in case he was lost in his murky madness. It wasn't even madness, as madness has a positive, energetic vibe to it. It was just a feeling of overwhelming 'ness'. A combination of numbness, otherness, wrongness, all wrapped up in an enormous jaggedness. Even when he felt he might be able to pretend to be alright, just to try to placate his expectant parents, he always knew that the depression was lurking somewhere in the air just behind him, waiting to drop on top of him and crush his fragile shape into a contorted amoeba of quivering vibrations.

The unpredictability was twofold. First because he never knew when the dangling depression might find him, but secondly, he never knew how long it would deign to take up residence. Such unpredictability rendered his life erratic and demanding. He preferred to be alone. At least if he were alone, he would not have to attempt to explain his condition and its behavioural spin offs to those around him.

He had done much reading about depression. However, understanding seemed to be of no use to him. It is generally accepted that learning and subsequent understanding helps the individual to come to better terms with most things. All his reading had done for him was to confirm what he already knew. Nothing could be done. Nothing could help. It was as if he shared his life with another. That his dangling depression frequently deigned to take up occupation in spite of himself. Oft-times such occupation would be total. In periods like this he could never find himself. Indeed, he would feel that he did not exist, or had ever existed. The dangling depression became omnipotent. At other times it was just visiting, almost like it was having a viewing of the body and deciding if it wanted to stay or not. Between these two extremes Mark had to manage his life. He was living a 'now you see me, now you don't' existence. At all times he had to try to control his being. It was exhausting. He had always felt that at times he was truly, a Lost Boy.

His intellect seemed to be able to cope with living within such confusion and uncertainty. He had done well at school. He had gained numerous qualifications. Academic rigour and linguistic ability were both easily achieved. He did well at university too, though he always kept himself to himself. He had no social life, nor any friends. He worked most of the time. He slept some of the time and the rest … well it was empty space. He filled it with nothing. Consequently, his emotional experience and his physical wellbeing were both compromised.

The two things which seemed to help him when he was recovering from a period of depression were reading the works of the Portuguese genius Fernando Pessoa and listening to Fado music. He would always have Pessoa's *The Book of Disquiet* by his bedside, along with CDs of a variety of Fado renditions. Pessoa's multiple personalities intrigued him, as did his divergent philosophical views on existence. Mark was impressed by the man's ability to translate emotion into words, thus enabling others to feel deeply. He wondered how the Portuguese had managed to hold the essence of emotion both in relation to poetic insights and musical transformations. The Portuguese were an old and developed nation which seemed to be able to mine the depths of global longing and rich emotional experience. Mark had thought for many years that perhaps the Portuguese had been the nation to fully understand the concept of passionate living. Their poetry and music would evoke the feeling of *saudade*, which symbolised irreparable loss and lifelong damage, a longing and passion for otherness. His understanding of such Portuguese *saudade* supported his fragile and tentative return to his life after his dangling depression had left. It would help him re-establish an emotional normality which was acceptable to his parents and even to himself. He would be able to continue and return to his studies supported by his understanding of the ramifications of Portuguese *saudade*. He would be able to feel again.

On finishing university, he returned to live with his parents. They were not happy with this arrangement though they would never tell him, or even admit it to themselves. His mother had also suffered with depression when she was younger. It seemed that any challenge to life experience would throw her into an inward spiral of turbulent turmoil. However, unlike Mark, she would usually have some idea as to the onset of such activity. Her doctor suggested that she had reactive depression. It seemed that she would react when things went wrong or when she was overwhelmed by life experiences. Fortunately, as she got older her depression appeared to decline, not only in frequency but in intensity too. This was all she could hope for in relation to expecting improvement for her son.

She found it very frustrating that he seemed to experience his dangling depression for no reason at all. She could not understand his condition as there seemed to be no cause for his dilemma. She always knew what caused her reactive depression. She felt he was using the depression to gain attention. This belief, along with the fact that she had limited affection for her son, meant that she had little time for him. She had not studied depression, consequently she had not understood that there are different manifestations and multiple causes as to the experience and onslaught of this chronic mental health illness. She was irritated that Mark did not act as she acted. That he did not manage his depression as she managed hers. The only way she could deal with her son's problems was to distance herself from him. This strategy worked well when Mark was at university, but his decision to return home following the completion of his courses caused her much concern.

On returning to the family home Mark did not have a job and he daily became more reclusive. Friends of his parents had noticed his many academic attributes and suggested that he join the civil service. His parents liked the idea and encouraged him to work for the civil service. They looked forward to the possible kudos of having a son who worked for the government. He applied and was invited for interview.

The interview date arrived. Prospective candidates would spend three days at a large country house in Berkshire. At all times they would be watched and monitored. The time was organised into different challenges and interactions. The results of the various tests and experiences would be recorded by the staff and organisers. Mark did not enjoy the interpersonal aspects of the weekend, but he relished the various test papers. He knew he would do well. He had always done well in exams, usually being top of his class in most areas of both verbal and non-verbal challenges. He felt comfortable. However, the times when he was forced to interact with his fellow candidates made him feel most uncomfortable. This was duly noted and recorded by the observers. The three days were completed. Mark felt confident that he would have done well on all the tests. He did not realise that academic ability was not the only thing being assessed.

He returned to his parent's house. They quizzed him about his experience. He told them he had done well and expected soon to be offered a place in the civil service echelons. He then retreated to his bedroom where he continued his self imposed solitude. Two days later he received a letter informing him that currently there was no position requiring his particular skills set. He was devastated. He did not tell his parents.

One of his lecturers at the university had previously told him that he thought the Government Intelligence Agency would offer a suitable work environment for him. At the time Mark had wondered what he had meant by 'suitable work environment'. Subsequently he had discussed this with the lecturer and discovered that using his language and mathematical skills, plus his desire to work alone, without interruption, would be possible at the Government Intelligence Agency. This lecturer had links with the headquarters and suggested that if Mark ever wanted any advice concerning applications and so on he would be happy to oblige. Mark remembered this and because of his rejection by the civil service had decided to contact the lecturer and seek his help. He made the phone call. He did not mention that he had been refused a place with the civil service. The phone call continued. It seemed the lecturer was keen to help.

One week later Mark was called for interview and given a job at the Government Intelligence Agency. He was amazed at the simplicity and speed with which he was accepted.

He told his parents. They feigned concern at him having to leave their home and move to Gloucestershire. He pretended being upset at having to leave them. All the while, Mark and his parents were surreptitiously delighted.

Mark moved into a flat in Cheltenham. He started his job and did well to establish his expertise very quickly. His flair for language and his ability to focus on tasks for hours on end meant he was soon promoted. He still was concerned about handling his dangling depression. If it hit, he would tell work that he had a cold, or had food poisoning. That was how he managed the periods when he could not attend work. Usually, he was able and willing to stay long hours. He enjoyed his work. His life continued in quite a balanced way for many years. Indeed, he had been well able to negotiate his life at the Government Intelligence Agency.

He had hoped that his dangling depression was like his mother's and would diminish as he aged. It appeared to be doing just that. Well, at least until the onslaught of falling in love. His falling in love with Jo. He knew that Jo was his soulmate. Jo was his very own Peter Pan and he was lost within his love of Jo. He listened on his phone, to Kelsey Ballerini as she sang 'Peter Pan'. How he loved the song. He felt his Peter Pan was escaping from Kelsey in order to come to him. Sadly he now knew he had been wrong. The adventure was over.

The trip to Hawaii and the catastrophic outcome of their last day together would have had a devastating effect on most people, but on Mark it appeared to be more dramatic, more insidious. It affected every aspect of his being. Jarring his coming to terms with his homosexuality, his understanding of his isolated world, his knowledge of his depressive state and his self esteem. The rejection caused all his understandings to dissolve and his self to fade into oblivion. His body took the hit too. His bones became dust as they crumbled beneath his skin. His blood thickened and congealed within his frozen veins. His organs screamed to be let out of his warring body, trying to escape the pain and atrophy, whilst his heart quietly began to shrink, finally contorting into a pin head of a misshape. Mark was lost. He had gone. 'Everybody Hurts' by R.E.M. played on the radio. This Lost Boy was finally completely lost. This boy had been abandoned by his very own Peter Pan.

Six months following his return from Hawaii found Mark sitting in a large communal lounge, within a private mental facility, on a hard sofa. He was facing an enormous window. The window overlooked ten tall silver birch trees rising above the numerous shrubs, which had been planted below to ensure privacy from the adjacent road. The wind was gentle, and the trees were moving to and fro, as if dancing like ballerinas for his pleasure. It was late afternoon but already stars could be seen appearing in the sky. There was music tickling the air as the shards of sunlight penetrated the glass and touched his body. It was as if the world was enticing him back. Trying to make him want to belong again. Trying to persuade his long dormant senses to return.

The first thing he saw was his knee. He became aware that he was looking at his knees. He was amazed to look at his knees. His eyes had been redundant for so long. Now they were looking again. They were looking at his knees. His head was drooped. That was why he could see his knees. His mind then registered that he was wearing brown needlecord trousers. Should he raise his head? Should he consider looking elsewhere? Would he be able to see other things apart from his knees?

He became fearful and excited at the same time. What was happening? Where was he? Should he be here? A flush of physical flutters rained on him. He knew he could see. He now knew he could feel too, he could feel the smooth softness of his corduroy trousers. He raised his head, yes, he could see out of the window, he could feel the sun on his arms. He listened, the music had changed. He could now hear the soft music of Chopin's 'Nocturn in E flat Major' caressing the air. He was still frightened, but this time he was frightened to move. Frightened that any movement would cause his awareness to retreat into the dark, silent void where it had lived for the past few months. He continued looking out through the window whilst he slowly, very slowly, sat upright. The sun had now fallen behind the trees and a groping darkness lurched across the skies, permeated only by miniscule pin pricks of intense light being thrown towards earth from friendly faraway stars.

A shadow encompassed his being as someone walked in front of him. They spoke.

'Are you alright?'

He made no response. The person before him called out across the lounge,

'Nurse, can you come quickly? I think something is happening to Mark.'

A few seconds later he felt someone touching his hand and asking again,

'Are you alright?'

He then heard his own voice exclaim, 'I am fine thank you.'

That was how Mark was restored to this world. The Lost Boy had been found. The Lost Boy had returned.

Mark remained still, not sure whether he wanted to return to this world or not. His previous childhood experience told him that he knew how to cope in situations like this. His parents and those around him had never really understood him. He had been forced to look elsewhere for his support and nurture. His childhood readings had helped him. He often entered Peter Pan's world. Peter seemed to understand him. Peter always knew what to do.

Mark closed his eyes, ignoring the nurse standing before him. Mark's mind returned to his childhood world. He soon found his friend Peter again. Peter explained that time was needed to sort what to do next.

> 'If you shut your eyes and are a lucky one, you may see at times a shapeless pool of lovely pale colours suspended in the darkness; then if you squeeze your eyes tighter, the pool begins to take shape, and the colours become so vivid that with another squeeze they must go on fire.'

Mark was ready to allow his flames to be fanned, he was ready to 'go on fire'. He knew in that moment that his inner fire would allow him to return to the world. It would light him enough to give him the courage to face people again. Eventually he hoped that it would allow him to fly.

He had always wanted to fly. When he was five, he had awoken from a deep sleep to be heralded by the thought 'You haven't flown for a long time'. His five-year-old sensibilities soon reframed his thinking. He knew people could not fly. Yet he questioned himself. If he could not fly, then how was it that he knew exactly what it felt like to fly? He even knew the problems he encountered with flying. His infant mind was telling him that he could not fly, yet his

body was telling him that he could. His mind tried to placate and soothe his body by acknowledging that it knew that
his body had had many problems when landing. He could
remember the difficulty he had on landing, when his feet,
or whatever was beneath him, had problems lowering themselves before hitting he ground. He also remembered being
laughed at by the beings around him. They would soar high
in the sky. They would swoop and do tumble overs. They
were happy and confident. He was not. He only flew just
above the tree line. He had never done a tumble over. He
was always being chastised and mimicked for his nervousness. Whatever the beings were, he was one of them. But he
was one of them who had problems flying. His infant mind
never ever sorted out what the beings were. The only person
in his parent's world, who would be able to understand was
Peter Pan. Peter could fly.

He remembered a line from *Peter Pan*:

> 'The moment you doubt whether you can fly, you
> cease forever to be able to do it.'

The five year old realised that he had lost his ability to fly.
Mark's doubt had stripped him of his abilities. He now
knew he would never fly again. His tiny body slumped into
sadness. He needed something to help him feel better. He
needed to be able to find something that he could do. His
flying had not been good. What could he do that he could
do well and that would make him feel better. It suddenly hit
him, as he asked Peter,

> 'If you cannot teach me to fly, teach me to sing.'

Singing had become part of Mark's life from the age of five.
He loved to sing. He had sung at home, at school, everywhere. He was good at singing. His singing was far superior

to his flying. He sung at every opportunity. He had sung until he had his first 'lost' period. His mum had called it 'his depression'. She had told him that he was 'just like her'. He was not sure how old he had been, but he knew he had gone somewhere else. He did not live in the world belonging to his mum and dad anymore. Eventually he had returned to their world, but he never sang out loud again. It was a sort of silent singing. Simon and Garfunkel had know about it when they wrote 'The Sound of Silence'. Mark's singing, following his depression, was never heard by anyone else. Mark only sang when he was alone and inside his own head. His silent being found succour in his inner music, within the sounds of his lonely silence.

He pondered his childhood wonders. He had flown before he was five but never since. He had started singing when he was five, but had never sung out loud since his first 'lost' period. He wondered if everybody had experienced similar childhoods. His logical mind thought that was not possible. He knew that most people could sing. He was the only person he knew who could not sing out loud.

He returned to his adult world. As he sat in the medical centre, wondering what to do next, his inner voice began to quietly sing. It was as if his inner voice knew he was thinking about it and had come out to play. He became comforted. He knew that eventually he would be able to sort everything out and return to his fragile reality. His inner fire was beginning to burn brighter.

He looked out of the window, the skies were completely dark and the stars smiled at him knowingly. He remembered …

'Stars are beautiful, but they may not take part in anything, they must just look on forever.'

Mark wished he were a star, but he knew he must take part in this life he had been given. He would need to leave Peter's world, he would need to negotiate his parent's world again but he would be comforted by his inner singing. His life could continue. The Lost Boy would be able to play the part of being a grown up again.

His consciousness was again thrust into the immediate surroundings of the ward where he had been living for the past six months. Bustle, noise, questions, activity and astonishment surrounded him. Doctors and nurses came and went. Vital signs were taken. Body parts were probed and measured. Questions were lobbed. He was being drowned in encouragement and euphoria. Those around him congratulated him and themselves at his remarkable and obvious recovery.

Two days later he was being discharged from the unit. His nurses were delighted to see him leave their effective cocooning care. The discharge was testament to their ability to manage mental health disorders.

His parents were not so delighted. Mark would need to live with them *pro tem*. Mark's feelings regarding his discharge were ambivalent. He did not want to remain in the unit. He wanted his freedom, yet he did not want to be elsewhere. He was fearful that elsewhere would not welcome him; that he would not be able to manage an elsewhere, wherever it was. He felt uncertain. It was time for him to leave. Time would sort things out. But time could be difficult,

'I suppose it's like a ticking crocodile, isn't it? Time is chasing after us all.'

His friend Peter, from his infancy, was helping him again. Mark knew he never wanted to return to the unit, and as Peter would always say,

'Never is an awfully long time.'

He also reassured Mark,

'So come with me, where dreams are born, and time is never planned. Just think of happy things, and your heart will fly on wings, forever in Never Never Land.'

But ...

'Take care, lest an adventure is now offered you, which if accepted, will plunge you in deepest woe. Once you have grown up you can't come back.'

Mark knew he must leave. He looked towards his new future with cold eyes whilst his inner song began. No one could hear him. His Grandma had taught him the song long ago. He had tried to find it on YouTube for her before she died. She knew it from an old 78 record her father had bought for her in the 1940s. He had not been able to find it on YouTube, except a foreign version. His Grandma knew all the English words.

'Naar de Speeltuin' by Heleentje van Capelle began in his head. Mark sang along, singing the English words his Grandma had taught him so long ago ...

'It was such a lovely dream. Quite the best I've ever seen. Worlds and worlds of wonderland. My eyes could not believe. It's a land far far away. Music there is always gay. We have so much fun. Oh, I wish you all could come.

It's a Never Never Land, with a Humpty Dumpty Band. Playing Ohla, Ohla, Ohla.

Everybody's in the band in the Never Never Land,
Playing Ohla, Ohla, Ohla.

You can jump across a moonbeam. You can swing
upon a star. You can even sit on rainbows shouting
Ohla from afar.

It's a Never Never Land with a Humpty Dumpty
Band. Playing Ohla, Ohla, Ohla all for you.'

Mark left the unit, with his Grandma's comforting song spi-
ralling around his brain. He knew he could not live in Never
Never Land. It was time to grow up.

CHAPTER SEVEN

JO'S SLOVAKIAN SOJOURN
– BEFORE COVID

'I've never done anything but dream. This, and this alone has been the meaning of my life. My only real concern has been my inner life.'

Fernando Pessoa, *The Book of Disquiet*

Jo needed to dream. His solitary being needed nurturing by his inner wonderings. Dreaming allowed him to function. Dreaming was his escape. Dreaming became his reality.

During his last days on Hawaii, he had been thrown into an internal quagmire. On some level, he had always known that for him, it was foolish to even consider a relationship. Nevertheless, he would dream of someday meeting someone, somewhere, somehow. On meeting Mark, his defences had been slowly broken down. He had been unconscious of any movement. Gradually, he had begun to let Mark invade his privacy and his awareness. Mark stealthily entered Jo's dream world by the back door.

Jo knew about his condition. He had read widely and realised that anyone with schizoid tendencies needs to be alone. They neither crave nor want relationships. They neither crave nor want society. They are loners.

Despite adopting a typical schizoid profile since receiving his diagnosis, he often wondered if perhaps the mental team he had worked with had been wrong. Psychiatrists can make mistakes. Maybe he was only slightly schizoid? Can anyone be slightly anything?

He was reminded of his reading about frog psychology and relationships. It was all nonsense he knew, but he did feel that possibly his relationship with Mark had been similar to the frog in the saucepan scenario. Apparently if you put a frog into a saucepan of cold water and increase the heat quickly, the frog jumps out. If you increase the heat slowly the frog doesn't realise, it stays in the saucepan and boils.

Mark had gradually insinuated his closeness into Jo's world. He had invaded Jo's space gradually. Jo had not seen Mark coming. He had not seen him coming until the kiss. The kiss so shocked Jo that he jumped! The heat had been turned up and Jo had to respond like the frog in hot water. Jo, the frog, had jumped. He just hoped no one else would kiss him. The saying 'you've got to kiss a lot of frogs before you find your prince' rang in his ears. He hoped no one would ever kiss him again. He did not want to become anyone's prince.

Now he needed to ensure that his life was back on track. On his solitary track which would allow him to avoid people and relationships. He wanted to return to the safety of his schizoid diagnosis. He found comfort in his label. He would not let anyone else inveigle their way gently into his world. His boundaries would be strong and fortified. His life would be safe. He would create his own narrative of solitude and self-reliance. He needed to escape from the Government Intelligence Agency and establish his new world order.

On the plane home from Hawaii, Jo had sent an email to the Government Intelligence Agency requesting a transfer. His request was unexpectantly soon granted. The Golden

Boy was an asset who needed to be nurtured; they did not want to lose him. He did not visit his headquarters again; all communications were via emails. His transfer was soon agreed and arranged.

Two weeks following his return from Hawaii saw Jo heading for Slovakia. Tensions had been rising in Ukraine since 2014. Intel was at a premium. Jo's linguistic and decoding skills were needed. He had been given a Slovakian flat in Poprad where he was to live undercover, as a drop out from the toxic western culture of capitalism. He could work out of the flat. He could travel to the Ukrainian border when instructed and meet with those working within Ukraine. He would be relatively safe in Slovakia. It was the perfect situation for him. Escape and a solitary existence were just what he needed after the demands of Hawaii. He knew Poprad was the gateway to the High Tatras Mountains. He would be able to pursue his love of outdoor activities and keep fit. He considered the move to be a useful transfer. A productive antidote to his previous dilemma.

His flat was small but bright. It was above a tea shop. He found the tea shop delightful. It was interesting and extensive. The front part of the shop was full of all sorts of paraphernalia associated with tea and tea making. All the walls were hung with shelves, and each shelf was stuffed full of brightly coloured teapots, infusers, cups and saucers, small heated samovars, mugs, spoons and extensive boxes of numerous different types of teas. Having entered the shop the customers had to deftly navigate their routes, passing all the tempting 'goodies' on the shelves before travelling through the narrow archway, at the rear of the shop, which led to the tea rooms. There were two interconnecting rooms, one furnished with tables and chairs, all brightly coloured in shades of turquoise and blues. The second room, accessed by another archway, exhibited numerous large velvet embroidered cushions of red, orange, ochre, ginger and pink. These cushions were scattered on the floor around several hubble bubble pipes. The walls were hung with various intricate Indian tapestries and carpets. The effect was that of a warm oriental oasis with exotic décor. The air was filled with spiced fragrances interspersed with occasional sharp thrusts of patchouli and ylang ylang oils. Eastern music added a mystical charm.

Menus were placed around the rooms. Menus was indeed a misnomer, they were more like booklets. The booklets, covered by gold embossed leather were held together by silken red and pink threads and decorative tassels. They contained insightful information regarding the over one hundred teas on offer. There were short paragraphs describing the various tea flavours but more importantly the different effects the varied teas would have on the body and in some cases, the mind. Jo always chose the tea which promised 'Release of internal tensions, and total inner peace.' Despite not ever noticing any 'release of internal tension' or any 'inner peace' he continued to order his favourite tea, and was always hopeful for some of the advertised responses. The tea shop also offered the perfect venue if he had to secretly meet any of his colleagues without causing any obvious attention.

He soon settled into his Poprad existence. Slovakia and his new assignment were good for him. New beginnings allowed him to forget old traumas. He could start afresh. He could escape from any real or imagined recriminations from Mark. He was safe.

Solitary sustenance and application to his work supported Jo as his life settled into the Slovakian hideaway.

Time stretched out before him as he slowly navigated a route through daily orders and expectations. Time seemed to gently push him away from his previous pain and anxiety towards a firmer grasp of his self-awareness. His mind became his own again. He promised himself that he would never let anyone near him ever again, socially, emotionally and most importantly physically. Jo felt that within his fragile body, Mark's abortive kiss had released more internal destructive energy than anything seen at Pearl Harbor. His reaction to Mark confirmed what he often wondered, he was not gay; yet he still felt that perhaps at some deep level he needed to be close to someone.

Whilst daily dealing with his inner world, Jo also knew that he needed to maintain his outer shell. His body was beautiful. He knew that such beauty needed maintenance and continuous care. He had intended to join a gym or swimming facility when he first moved to Slovakia. What he found in Poprad was far in excess of what he needed or desired. AquaCity was a large complex of pools, saunas, steam rooms, gyms and bars. He had never seen anything like it before. Its sheer size gave it the added bonus of allowing Jo to find places where he could be almost alone and away from most people. He immediately became a member and started his daily workouts. The place would close at ten in the evening. If Jo worked out from eight till nine, he could then swim until nine forty-five before having to shower and leave. Most people had left the facility earlier. One of the smaller pools, near the men's changing room was almost always free of people. He began to consider it as 'Jo's Pool'. His daily trips to AquaCity allowed him the exercise and cleanliness he needed and craved.

Jo's time in Slovakia seemed to be allowing him to heal and find a new, unchallenged way of living. Unchallenged by his own inner thoughts as well as any demands made by others. Life was good. Living within his acceptance of his schizoid label was comfortable. However, he still had that nagging doubt whether he was truly living a real and authentic life. Whilst not wanting to disturb his so recently found equilibrium, he nevertheless kept wondering if perhaps his diagnosis had been wrong. He knew typical schizoids would show no interest in sex with another. Indeed, he had had no interest in any interpersonal sexual encounters for much of his previous life. He asked himself if his response to Mark's kiss had been because he did not want to be kissed or was it that he did not want to be kissed by a man. He had never had to wonder if he was straight, homosexual, bisexual or asexual. He knew that most teenagers would try to fathom their way towards self-acceptance of their own sexuality. He had never had to even consider it. His schizoid label had removed his need to think. He had accepted that he did not want or desire any form of sexual, indeed interpersonal closeness. So why was he thinking about it now? Why had Mark's kiss so upset him? Why was he questioning his own feelings which he thought he had sorted out years before? He decided to turn the volume down in his mind and log all his questions in that part of his brain which he labelled 'to be dealt with later'.

Jo's life fell into a gentle rhythm. He was undertaking all the demands sent to him from the Government Intelligence Agency. He was managing his hidden solitary life well. Time passed and he became settled in his Slovakian sojourn. Any thoughts that entered his head regarding his sexuality, Mark or his schizoid tendencies, were quickly dismissed or placed in his ever expanding 'to be dealt with later' file.

His 'later' was to be thrust on him sooner than he realised. His 'later' was to devastate his gentle way of life and insist on him opening his file in order to answer all the questions that had been accumulating within. His 'later' had become his 'now'.

Jo sat quietly and began to consider what had happened to him. He would often try to observe his life as if he were an onlooker. A voyeur considering his past. He began creating his own narrative, telling himself a story which would help him come to terms with his different realties. He took some paper and began writing his tale …

It was a Saturday night and as usual the AquaCity was pulsating with eager young bodies enjoying the delights of swimming, drinking and water dancing. Martha and the Vandelas were screaming 'Dancing in the Street.' Perhaps 'Dancing in the Pool' would have been more appropriate. Nevertheless, Martha's beat and the dynamic musical excitement were only too evident for those dancing in the shared waters. Most people were in couples, mostly heterosexual couples, though there were the odd individuals like me. I looked around and felt sad that obviously there was no room for any overt LGBTQ community to share in the enjoyment. It seemed that neurotypical heterosexuals had no idea of the gifts they had already received. The world was made for them. They easily fitted into it. Whilst I was still not sure what sexual label I wanted to attach to myself, I nevertheless felt unease knowing that some members of the LGBTQ community would feel excluded from many social gatherings, including Saturday Night Date Fest at AquaCity. Slovakian society was slow to catch up with sexual sensibilities supposedly accepted in the West. The Saturday night Fun Fest had begun, but I was not part of it.

My needs were basic. I needed to exercise and swim to expel some of the tensions that had built up within my body during my visits across the border to Kiev. The situation had been getting more volatile. I was supposed to be a sleeper. Things had been easy for quite a while but now I was unsure. My contacts were beginning to fear meeting me. I was not getting the information or feedback I needed. Consequently, Head Office was not happy with my reports. I felt ineffectual and at the same time quite fearful of my position, both professionally and personally.

Though I needed to be in the water, I did not want to have to experience the noise, closeness and fun of the main pool. I felt that the strobe lights and the dancing laser beams were enough to make most people feel nauseous. I walked away from the colourful lighted areas towards my quiet pool near the men's changing rooms. The pool was empty and the lights had been dimmed. No one was expected to be in this pool at this time in the evening. The pool was mine. I slipped slowly into its refreshing waters. My body sighed through every pore as my arms pulled me through the sensuous water. I could still hear some of the music from the main pool area, but it seemed quelled and far off. They were playing Ed Sheeran's 'Perfect'. I realised that the music heralded a time for slow mellifluent beats to enhance the closeness of the numerous couples in the building, moving them towards a more sensual atmosphere. I felt a slight twinge of, not jealousy, but inquisitive enviousness, knowing I did not have the capacity, or the wish, to experience such closeness nor the ability to feel such sensuality.

I just continued to swim my lengths up and down in total solitary enjoyment. I was being seduced by the water. I needed nothing more than feeling its ripples along my sides and over my skin. I was reminded of a beautiful poem by DH Lawrence where he describes the life of a fish as being 'a sluice of sensation along his sides'. I was fishlike. I could easily have been a fish. I did not want to have to endure the problems of relationships, or people or even sex. If I had been a fish I would have been totally happy. Fish have no need to consider anything but their own existence. Fish don't have to worry about reports, or whether Head Office is happy or not. A fish just enjoys being.

I sent a small prayer upwards, requesting any future reincarnations to be in the shape of a large trout. Yes, that would be acceptable. Not only would I be able to spend days just swimming alone but there would be the added fun of the periodical jumps upstream to enhance my activities.

As I was beginning to relax and know that my body was returning to some semblance of normality after the recent strains and stresses, I noticed that a woman was sitting on the edge of the pool just watching me. She had not been there when I arrived, so she must have come quietly to the pool as I swam up and down. I am used to people watching me. I know that at times my dress and my make-up would set me up for attention. But here I was not dressed and I certainly was not wearing any make-up. She just kept looking at me. She did not smile. She did not speak. She just stared.

I began to feel uncomfortable, though I did not stop swimming. I continued ploughing up and down the pool for another several minutes. She did not move, nor did she avert her gaze. She wanted me to know that I was being watched. It was a strange inter-action. I felt confusion. I neither needed nor craved attention. Any attention women had given to me in the past had made me uncomfortable. But this was different. This woman was unusual. She continued to watch me. I surreptitiously tried to look at her out of the corner of my eye as I swam past. She was about four metres away from me at my nearest swimming point. It was difficult to make out any details. But I did note that her skin was sun kissed. Her long hair which fell over her shoulders in curls, was a deep auburn tinged with gold. She wore a vibrant green one-piece swimming costume and her limbs were long and athletic. Perched on the top of her head was a pair of green glasses which she seemed to be using as a head band to hold the profusion of her locks away from her face. I remembered my reading about Dorothy searching for the Wizard when she had been transported to the magical word of Oz:

'He opened the big box, and Dorothy saw that it was filled with spectacles of every size and shape. All of them had green glass in them. The Guardian of the Gates found a pair that would just fit Doro-thy and put them over her eyes.'

It was too dim for me to notice any facial details, but my first impressions were that she was quite beautiful, if not enigmatic. She seemed bewitching. I was beginning to get a bit tired. I had exerted myself enough for one evening. Indeed, my vanity had forced me to extend my strokes and thrusts through the water in order to impress the angelic sylph who was watching me. I began to question myself. Why was I doing this? Why did I want to impress this shadowy figure observing me from the side of the pool? I had never needed or even wanted attention before. There was a strange pleat in my personality which hid any need for attention. What was happening to me? My body began to feel tingly. Was I beginning to feel arousal? I began to question my schizoid label again.

As I slowed down and thought that I should leave the water, I noticed that she raised herself from where she had been sitting and moved away into the shadows. She was gone. I closed my eyes tightly, wishing her to return. She did not. All I could do was to try to remember her. I let my inner eye pull pictures into my consciousness. The first thing it delivered was a view of her green glasses. The glasses on her head had reminded me of the colour of Oz. It was called emerald green. I decided to call her my Enchantress. My thoughts then returned to the Wizard of Oz. Had not Dorothy worn green glasses? Was not Oz bathed in green light? AquaCity had been transformed into the Emerald City. My beautiful siren must have been a descendant of Dorothy's. I let my mind play with the fantasy, and then I forced it to return to the moment. I hoped I would see her again.

I pulled my well exercised body from the pool and taking my towel I walked towards the male shower rooms. They were empty. Everyone else was still enjoying the fun and frolic in the main pool area. I entered the first shower cubicle on the left. Throwing my towel over the shower door and facing the back wall, I turned the water dial to hot. Immediately I was covered in sharp needles of invigorating water. The rhythms from the dancing music continued. My body moved from side to side as the music enticed me into a physical euphoria. I became like a whirling dervish attempting to move towards spiritual serenity. I felt so energised. I reached out to push the level which released the gel from the wall mounted container. As I did so I heard a noise behind me and simultaneously I felt two arms around my waist, then a body was being pressed into my back. I knew it was her. I did not move. I placed my two arms in front of me, steadying myself against the pale green tiled wall. She continued to press into my body. I could feel her skin along the entire length of my back, buttocks and legs. She was almost as tall as me. She pressed her body into mine whilst her arms entangled my torso. She had some sort of gel in both her hands. I could smell it. It was a smell I knew well. I had always loved Chanel's L'Eau Savage. Her adept hands ran across my stomach and downwards towards my thighs. She continued rubbing her sweet-smelling gel into my skin and delighting my senses. Still, I did not move. I had never experienced anything like it in my life before. I did not know what was happening to me. I was a bewildered and compliant new incarnation. I was totally overcome with not just physical but emotional extravagance. My breathing became laboured and heavy as she continued to gently stroke every part of me that she could reach. I did not move … I just let myself give in … I surrendered. We neither of us spoke, listened nor looked. It was as if we both knew that in order to maintain the heightened feelings which we were experiencing; we needed to ignore all other senses. To disregard all other sensations. Touch, her tantalising and tempting touch was all that was necessary to create a spell of sensual delirium. We had both moved into a state of enchantment. We were entangled in an emerald enchantment.

My eyes were closed. My nostrils filled with perfume, her perfume. My body was aching under her eloquent hands. I breathed in deeply. As I did so, she released me. I shivered and quaked. I could not move for a few seconds and when I could … she had gone. I continued to use the shower walls as support. I was totally overcome with all sorts of strange and new emotions. However, my major emotion seemed to be one of disbelief. I knew me. I knew I did not want nor need sex. But what had happened to me in the shower was beyond sex. It was a magical esoteric transformation. I would never be the same again. This woman had transported me beyond myself. Her seduction had thrust my being into a world I had never imagined. I glowed in the ecstasy of it all. A green glow reflected from the tiles and cascaded around me. I had been transported to the magical world of Oz. I had been enchanted. AquaCity had become my Emerald City …

'... a bright green glow can be seen far off into the distance many miles away that shines brightly high up, above the city and into the sky even in broad daylight. The closer you get to the city, the more its glow intensifies, and becomes brighter and brighter until everything surrounding the city, including the rays of the sun appear to be of a greenish tint.'

I had found my Enchantress with green glasses but where was she now?

She had gone. Where was she? I had not even seen her. She had always been behind me. What did she look like? What colour were her eyes? Would I recognise her again? What would I recognise? Where would I find her?

I draped my towel around my waist and walked out of the changing rooms looking for her as I went. I soon encountered numerous bodies moving towards me. The crowd had left the main pool and was now entering the changing rooms. The Saturday night Fun Fest had ended. The music continued whilst everyone left the main pool area and sought their clothes and towels. I could hear the Latin rhythms of Camila Cabello, singing 'Don't Go Yet', blasting through the speakers. I wished my sylph hadn't gone. She had not listened to Camila's instructions. She HAD gone. I knew I would never find her amidst all the laughing bodies surrounding me as they danced to the music whilst preparing to leave. They were ecstatic, copying all the hand and hip movements of Camila's video which could be seen on the screens placed around the complex. It was a scene of fun and pure frivolity. Everyone seemed happy. Sadly, the happiness did not touch me. I was distraught and dejected. She had disappeared and I had been abandoned. I had lost my Emerald Enchantress.

The only thing I could do was to step away from my rapturous encounter in the shower and return to the reality of my flat. One hour later saw me sitting in bed with my hands in my head, trying to conjure what had happened to me. My head was working, but my body was discombobulated. My body was overcome by her tingling and tantalising treatment. My body was screaming at my mind wanting to know what had happened, and when would it happen again? Arguments and confusions continued to bounce between my mind and my body. It was all getting to be too dramatic. Sleep would be my only course of action. Sleep would allow time for my mind and my body to reconnect and reconcile their differences. My established schizoid mind and my emergent sexual body needed sleep so that I could accommodate their differences. Sleep came. Sleep came to the rescue.

Jo breathed deeply as he finished creating his personal narrative. His mind returned to the here and now.

The next morning allowed Jo to return to the mundane realities of his work life in Slovakia. Everything was beginning to become dangerous. Jo knew he had to leave. The escalation of the conflict between Russia and Europe surrounding the situation in Ukraine meant that he and most of his colleagues were being pulled out. He was being sent to Djibouti, a strategic East African country on the Horn of Africa. As usual, his linguistics skills would be needed. He had been to Djibouti once before, though he did not enjoy it. His usual calm compliancy made him overlook the possibility of experiencing difficulties surrounding access to food and material goods. Djibouti imported most of its food. There was limited agriculture due to climatic conditions but some animal husbandry. The nomadic Afar people would settle along the coast or around the low lying salt lake district of Lac Assai. Food was at a premium, whilst natural resources like salt, perlite and marble were used for export. The US had established a strategic base at Djibouti at the turn of the century with access to both the airport and seaport facilities. It was the only permanent US base in Africa and had been established due to the geopolitical positioning near Sudan, Kenya and Uganda. Other countries had soon realised the importance of the country to the international shipping trade network. Japan and China had also established overseas military installations with economic support becoming a major consideration.

Jo felt indifferent about the move. Though he did have some reservations, he knew he would have to leave soon. Life in Slovakia and Ukraine was becoming more problematic by the day. Djibouti called. Despite being aware of the global problems that were simmering, Jo had one major concern which seemed to dwarf any work issues. This major concern focused on his Enchantress. He wondered how he would find her and when he would see her again. He could not get her out of his thoughts. She had put a magical spell on him. His ruminations all revolved around her and only her. His enticing Enchantress had taken over his mind.

He was now entangled in an emerald enchantment, and he did not know how to escape.

CHAPTER EIGHT

RELATIONSHIPS AND FRAGMENTATION

'You know that place between sleep and awake, that place where you can still remember dreaming? That's where I will always love you.'

JM Barrie, *Peter Pan*

Jo had awoken early. His sleep had indeed calmed some of his inner turmoil. Yet his thoughts continued to revolve around her. Despite not even knowing her name, or what she looked like, he now knew two important facts about his being. He knew that he could experience sexual feelings and he knew he was on the brink of experiencing a relationship. The only thing he didn't know was who had awakened his sexual feelings and who he might be in a relationship with?

It seemed as if as soon as he unpicked the mystery of one area of his existence another area of unknowns emerged. He lay still in his comfortable bed as he began to review his position. He forced his mind towards a clinical analysis of the situation. He listened to his own self crafted internal report, as he tried to clarify and depersonalise what had happened to him ...

He had been living in Slovakia since he asked for a transfer on his return from Hawaii. He had been sent there in order to help monitor the volatile situation between Russia and Ukraine. His command of languages was necessary to converse with other surveillance operatives working in the area. He had taken a small studio flat in the town of Poprad. He had originally been ordered to Kosice but he felt that as it was the second largest town in the country it would be the obvious place for others to look for recent newcomers. He wanted to remain hidden. He needed to be able to move freely between Slovakia and Ukraine. Also there seemed to be more of a transient tourist community in Poprad. He could remain undetected and not draw attention to himself. It was agreed with his superiors. He could stay in Poprad.

Poprad was the location of AquaCity. He needed to swim. Swimming was second nature to him. It allowed him to forget the demands of his body. To forget the confusion of his amorphous personality. To relax and to reform after many challenging interactions. Swimming held his molecules and his fragmented mind together. The pools in AquaCity enhanced his existence, allowing him to function and appear outwardly like most neurotypicals.

He had wondered about his status as a neurodivergent, indeed a schizoid personality. He had settled into work and a placid solitary existence. Life had been progressing well. Until one Saturday night in AquaCity, when he had encountered his Enchantress wearing an emerald green swimsuit, and with her glasses perched on the top of her head. One chance encounter had changed his life forever.

Jo stopped his inner reporting and got out of bed. He knew it was imperative that he return to his mundane everyday reality. He made a coffee and decided that the only course of action was to try to find her. He needed to know who she was. Where she lived. What she was doing in Poprad. He needed to find her; he needed to see her again. He closed his eyes and longed to feel her touch, he ached to feel her touch.

The next evenings saw Jo swimming in his quiet pool as usual. The only difference in his visits now that he was searching for her was that he would visit the other pools in the complex. He would watch all the other swimmers. He was looking for her.

She could not be found. He searched for six days. He was getting more and more anxious. Supposing he could not find her? Supposing she had left the country? Supposing she … his last supposing was unthinkable. This last supposing made him fear that perhaps the whole episode had not happened. Had his fragile yet creative brain conjured it all? Was it all a devious mind game playing with his emotions and feelings? Had he been hallucinating? Was his atypical brain playing Machiavellian chess with him?

Another day arrived. He slowly walked in the direction of the City. His gait was laboured. He did not know what to do. He felt lost and alone. He had always flourished at being alone. Now it seemed that she had even taken his aloneness enjoyment away from him. He wanted to be with another; he wanted to be with her. To feel her, to know her. His life was beginning to revolve around her … this Emerald Enchantress with no name.

He stopped his internal assessment of how he had met her. He needed to do something to try to find her. He continued walking towards the City which loomed before him. He entered the building, changed and was soon submerged in his favourite pool. He began swimming up and down, forging through the water as he forced his body into movement. Then, as he turned towards yet another pained lap, he suddenly saw her. She was sitting in the same position as when he had first discovered her. Shock caused him to stall in the water, and then he swam eagerly in her direction. As he approached, she smiled. He could make out her face. He sought her features. He wanted to absorb and remember every part of her visage. Her eyes thrust through him. They were dark and fearsome. He felt their intensity as his spine chilled with expectancy. She then suddenly raised her body and swiftly moved away. He watched her green swimsuit fade into the shadows as she moved towards the changing rooms. Just as before her green glasses were perched casually on her head. He watched his Green Enchantress move away from him. He had no choice but to follow. He exited the pool and quickly entered the changing rooms. He looked around, and then moved towards the first shower.

She was already there, waiting for him. The fragrance of L'Eau Savage entered his nostrils as he moved towards her naked body. They met. At last he could look at her. She was more beautiful than he had imagined. Their eyes met with an intensity he had never felt before. Her dark eyes seemed to pull him into her, forcing his being to flow towards her and to become encased within her gaze. Neither moved. They just stared into each other's soul, then slowly smiled with a shared understanding of the wonderland they were about to enter. She reached out to him, pulling him towards her as they became entwined in a frenzy of pent-up emotions and needs. They clung to each other, they became entangled, not knowing which parts belonged to which body. Ecstasy and enjoyment released them and thrust them into a different world. They had found each other and had escaped, leaving this world behind them. They had created a new world together.

Jo looked again into her penetrating eyes. There was a strange depth to the way she looked at him. He was mesmerised by her stare. He was enchanted. AquaCity had become Oz's Emerald City and unlike Dorothy, neither of them wanted to find their way home. They would remain in the glorious emerald greenness of Oz. The music system was playing 'Give a Little Bit' by Supertramp. Jo listened. He jokingly said to her 'a little bit is not enough. It must be in excess or not at all'. The song continued. She had looked into his lonely eyes wanting to see his smile, wanting to take his hand, wanting to be surprised. The song said it all. The song ended as they kissed and she left the cubicle.

So that was how Jo found her and that was how they started their life together.

Her name was Martina. She enjoyed being with Jo. She found his aloof aloneness tantalising. She wanted to be with him. Having initially unlocked his previously crippled sexual awareness she had become amazed at how easily he had been able to please her. She knew she was sexually experienced. She knew what she wanted. She would always be in control and move any activity towards suiting her particular needs. Most people would follow her lead. But with Jo it was different. Jo seemed to know instinctively what she wanted and how to please her. She did not need to coerce Jo into specific actions or to make demands upon him. He appeared to understand her needs and to be well able to fulfil them. She felt comfortable in the knowledge that he was enthralled by her. She could tell by the way he looked at her that she had conquered his mind. She possessed him. She would be able to maintain his interest for as long as she needed him. He would not leave her. She would not be abandoned.

At last, she felt she had found her soul mate. All her years of deception and falsehoods towards supposed conquests, who she hoped might fulfil her needs, seemed to melt into her staccato past. Now she seamlessly could hope for a new future, a future of sexual satisfaction and closeness. This man would not leave her. This man needed her and at last she had found someone who she needed too. Life would be good. She had discovered her King. Her verdurous King. Everything, this time, would be perfect.

The next few weeks saw our two 'lovebirds' meeting every evening in their pool at AquaCity. The venue for their developing affair suited them both. Martina enjoyed working at the centre. Part of her job description was to choose all the music which was relayed throughout the building. Martina knew the power of music and how it could be used to manipulate people. She liked to be able to manipulate people. Another reason why Martina enjoyed working in the City was because it was always clean and well organised. She had a tight timetable which ensured that she knew exactly what was expected of her at any moment. She enjoyed order and cleanliness. Her meetings with Jo would always be clinical in their simplicity. The showers allowed them privacy and cleanliness. A sterile environment for their evolving sexuality and frivolous fantasies to be played out. She was having fun. She was not bored. This man could please her. She had found her soul mate. At last, she felt safe.

Jo had been bowled over by meeting his Enchantress. She had lured him into a world he had never needed, indeed had never known existed. Lured is perhaps the wrong word. She had trapped him in his shower and thrown an invisible net of desire over his recently cleansed body. She had overwhelmed him physically. She had touched parts of him which he had not known existed. She had opened him to a new understanding of his body and its potential. But more than just a physical awakening, she had also allowed his mind to be released. To be released into another world. A world of her making.

Jo would sit in his flat and delight in just imagining what she looked like. What she felt like. Who she was. Jo asked Alexa to play 'Lifted' by the Lighthouse Family as he watched the raindrops slide down the window pane. He was longing for her.

His more practical thoughts reinforced what he knew about her. She was in charge. She was in control. She easily invaded his limited narrative and gave him another expansive area in which to play. Jo felt overwhelmed and happy. He would never have found this part of himself on his own. She had been able to fulfil his innermost desires and urges which, for too long, had ached to be recognised. At last Jo knew all his previous understandings would need to be reformed in the light of his desire for this special woman, his magical Enchantress with green glasses. He was well and truly obsessed.

For days every evening was spent at the centre. Martina would give Jo tokens of love which cost nothing. Small hand pressed flowers, a purple teasel, a tiny quilted golden heart filled with lavender. She would also woo him with poetry. She encouraged him to look at the poetry of Rumi, saying it was romantic and intoxicating. She shared her favourite lines from Rumi,

> 'Your task is not to seek for love, but merely to seek and find all the barriers within yourself that you would have built against it.'

'Be grateful for whatever comes, because each has been sent as a guide from beyond.'

She told Jo that he should read *The Forty Rules of Love: A Novel of Rumi* written by Elif Shafak. In the novel, Shafak states how 'difficult it is to love fellow human beings with all their imperfections and defects.' Whilst not understanding much of the spiritual elements in the novel herself, Martina knew the concepts would resonate with Jo's philosophical and spiritual understandings. Martina was well versed in the art of love-bombing. She knew how to captivate Jo's mind.

Gradually, Martina began to feel more confident and more able to know that Jo would accept any demands that she would make. At last, she felt she could see Jo again and again. She would not grow bored. He would always be pleased to see her. He would never chastise her. He would always play the games she desired and needed. He managed to supply her every need. She felt elated and overjoyed. Her life became manageable and fun. She knew that Jo was someone who would ignore her imperfections and defects. Jo would love her. At last, she felt she may be able to feel close to another. To feel intimacy.

All her life intimacy had been an enigma to her. Usually when she felt she was on the verge of understanding what intimacy felt like, feelings of fear would overwhelm her and she would back away. She did not want to be engulfed by another. She needed her own space which she alone could control. Jo never tried to get too close to her. He always seemed distant. He would not engulf her.

Neither Jo nor Martina needed any intrusions into their fantasy worlds. They were spinning around each other at a distance which allowed them both to feel comfortable.

There was no room for anything or anyone else. The invisible magnetic field they maintained between their separate beings allowed them to flourish. The distance was as important as the closeness. The distance created a vortex which allowed them to continue encircling each other, side by side yet apart.

This vortex of various ever-expanding desires and discoveries fed them both. They needed nothing else. Christina Perri's 'A Thousand Years' resonated from the music system. They were becoming entangled. Step by step every meeting brought them closer to each other.

Jo was overwhelmed, but also aware enough to realise that the seduction and secrecy of their relationship was well able to continue within his hidden world of work. His life needed to be hidden. Others would try to invade his space, wanting more, wanting information, wanting to know about him. Martina was different. Martina never needed to question him about his life. She did not appear interested. He did not need to hide his reasons for being in Slovakia. She just accepted him as she found him and never asked him any questions regarding his life or his work. She really was just not interested. All she needed was his daily presence and his availability. What he did when he was not with her was of no consequence. She neither cared nor wondered what he did with the rest of his time so long as he fulfilled her needs each evening. For her the arrangement was perfect, so long as Jo supplied what she needed when she needed it. She was happy with her King, and he was happy with his Enchantress.

Eventually Jo began to realise that their interactions were not like those he had viewed between the people he had observed at work; people who were supposedly 'in love' or 'going steady'. He knew she was different, not just because she had transgressed into his psyche and taken over his long dormant desires, but because she required nothing of his emotional being. Indeed, he was self-aware enough to understand that part of his attraction to her was because all she needed was his physical being. His fear of involvement or closeness was not a concern to him anymore. She did not want or require involvement or closeness. His body was enough. She wanted a playmate. When she found him and showed him the games she wanted to play he was initially forced to join in. Then on realising that he enjoyed the physical superficiality of their interactions, he was able to relax in the knowledge that she would demand nothing further from him. He could supply what she needed at no cost to himself.

Jo had always tried to understand his way of being, to reflect upon his feelings and reactions. He knew his schizoid label acted as a structure helping him to negotiate his world. He would often wonder at the correctness of his label. Now, following the unlocking of his sexual self he wondered if perhaps he needed more. Would he want and be able to manage a relationship? Would he want and be able to give more than just physical fulfilment? Could he enjoy an expanding emotional closeness with his wonderful siren? His schizoid self was being invaded by a different, a more inclusive personality. He felt he was able to change, indeed he felt he was changing. Personalities can change he told himself. He wondered if such a statement was in fact true. Can personalities really change?

He began to consider his interactions with Martina again. He wondered why all their meetings took place in AquaCity. He made a conscious decision to expand their physical world. A decision which would test his resolve to try to develop a deeper closeness between them. He would ask Martina when her next day off would be and he would suggest a trip into the High Tatra mountains or over the border into Austria, where they could walk and enjoy the scenery. He wanted to share the outside world with his siren. He wanted to show her the wonders of nature that had always been so nurturing to his previously uncomfortable soul. He wanted to be closer and to share his world with hers.

Little did he realise the ramifications of his innocent requests. He was about to unleash a chain reaction much like those created at CERN, during an experiment with nuclear fusion. Physically transplanting their world beyond AquaCity would render them both challenged, possibly challenged beyond their capabilities.

Jo decided how he would approach Martina with his request. Thus, many weeks after their initial meeting, Jo asked Martina if she would accompany him on a visit to the High Tatras where they could walk around the lakes. His request caused much discomfort within Martina's mind. She liked to always be in control, and that meant being in the centre. She did not want to leave the cleanliness and comfort of AquaCity. She could always control the situation as long as they remained in the City. She would not be fearful, so long as she knew her surroundings.

At first, she used delaying tactics to placate Jo's invitations, saying the weather was about to change and that it would be better to await a more settled period before attempting to walk in the High Tatras. She lied as she explained that she could not visit Austria as she did not possess a passport. These reasons seemed acceptable to Jo. However, after several days of fairly rational reasons, Jo recognised that she was using evasive excuses. Martina did not want to leave the security of the AquaCity complex.

Jo was disappointed but his need for her meant that he decided not to press her any further. He stopped asking her if they could travel on her days off. He just settled into their daily routines. Their lives continued together ... together each evening. Nothing else mattered. Jo was reminded of Metallica's song 'Nothing Else Matters'. Like Metallica, he knew he could not give her any more from the heart than he had already given. He was also beginning to realise that she did not want to develop their meetings into a relationship. She just wanted him to be her sexual playmate.

Their evenings of entwined lives continued. Everything revolved around the meetings in the showers. They would not meet anywhere except AquaCity and the focus of the meetings would always be upon their physical interactions. Jo's wanting to develop a relationship and to move their world beyond the City was stalled.

One evening, as they moved away from the pool area, Jo managed to get her to enter the photo booth situated in the entrance to AquaCity. He had pushed her gently towards the booth. She had refused to have her photo taken with him, but had agreed that he could have a photo of her. He could keep it near to his heart when he was not with her. She had heard such romantic nonsense on a TV programme. Jo seemed to like the idea, agreeing that he would always keep her photo with him.

Their meetings continued. Nothing changed and nothing else mattered. It all appeared manageable, until one cool autumnal Sunday evening when Jo received notification that his time in Poprad would be coming to an end. He had known that he would have to leave Slovakia sooner or later.

But now it seemed the time had come. He would have to leave at the end of the month.

It appeared that his skills were no longer needed in Slovakia. The situation was volatile causing the Government Intelligence Agency to request that he leave Poprad and travel to Djibouti. Jo knew very little of the place, which was part of the horn of Africa. He had been sent to the American base there once but only for two days. The Americans had needed a linguist with skills in Somali, Afar, Arabic and French. Jo was the perfect operative for the job. The base was extensive. He had been overcome by its sheer size. He had stayed in the part of the American base which accommodated visiting foreign naval officers. It was noisy, hot, smelly and generally dirty. He disliked being there and longed to leave and return to England.

He pondered the move. Normally he would be quite comfortable to move to pastures new. He enjoyed new challenges. He knew he would be working undercover within the community. He would not have to visit the American base. Nevertheless, his reaction to the news was far from his usual response. He felt overwhelmed with confusion and concerns. He could not leave and travel to Djibouti. He could not leave his Enchantress. How would he manage without her? He needed to be near her.

Most people feel concern at being separated from loved ones. The anxiety and dismay that Jo felt was far beyond any normal response to separation. The more he considered being away from her the more distraught he became.

He wondered what to do. He knew he would have to leave. He decided that the only course of action would be to take her with him. She would have to move too. At the same time, he also realised that it would be almost impossible to get her to accompany him. She would not even go into the Tatra Mountains with him. She would not leave the confines of AquaCity. How was he going to persuade her to move to another country? Another country which he knew little about. Also, she had told him that she did not even possess a passport.

He reviewed his situation. He was aware enough to know that part of his success at the Government Intelligence Agency was linked to his demeanour. His need to be alone and to refuse social interactions had been viewed as an asset. He felt that taking her to Djibouti might be problematic. He needed time to manage the situation. He also needed time to persuade Martina to accompany him. He needed to get her a passport. A British passport. He had contacts. He had her photo. He knew he could get her a passport in a few days, at a cost. He decided to get her a new passport. He would use the name Green. She liked green. He decided he would get her a passport with the name Martina Green. He found the idea amusing. It would be a surprise for her.

Two weeks later saw Jo and Martina meeting as usual. They swam together listening to the piped music. The rhythms of the music pulsed through their bodies, linking them at an organic level. It was an evening much like the many evenings they had already spent together. After they had swum, they moved towards the shower block. Everything was progressing as usual. They seemed both happy and fulfilled. But seeming and being are two different things. Jo was churning inside. He knew he had to share the news of his departure with Martina. He only hoped she would see the sense of her joining him in Djibouti. He hoped she would be amused by having a passport in the name of Martina Green.

The time had come for him to tell her about his transfer. They left the showers and Jo pulled her gently towards the concrete seats which had been erected around the pool area. It was late. The City would be closing in half an hour. He sat her down. Smiled and told her his news. She looked vacantly at him. She seemed to be unable to understand the magnitude of what he had said. He repeated himself.

'I will have to leave Slovakia at the end of the month. There is nothing I can do to change the situation. My work necessities me having to leave.'

She still sat unmoved.

'Here I have a present for you.' Jo tried to involve her in what he was saying.

He handed her the passport. She still looked bemused. She did not smile. She turned the passport pages slowly. He wondered if perhaps she did not like the name Green. Or perhaps she hadn't realised that he wanted her to accompany him to Djibouti. Before he could add any sweeteners or any thought of asking her to join him in Djibouti she stood up and moved quickly away from him. He was left sitting alone whilst she walked quickly towards the ladies' changing rooms.

She had gone. He sat for a while wondering what to do. Though she would regularly join him in the men's changing rooms he knew he could not follow her into the female changing rooms, he was too inhibited. All he could do was to return to the men's changing rooms and get ready to leave. This he did.

When he was dressed and ready for the outside world he moved towards the exit at the front of the City. There was still no sign of her. He looked around, knowing that she would have to be somewhere in the vicinity. He moved purposefully around all the various pools and bar areas. He could not find her. The place was shutting down. Two of the security guards smiled and gesticulated towards the exit door.

Jo left the building and returned to his flat.

He did not know where she was. He did not know what to do. Jo felt as if part of him had been wrenched from his body and thrown into another being. He had never felt like it before. He had never experienced such emotional pain. He realised that if being separate from her for such a short time made him feel so lost, moving to another country and being away from her was something he would not be able to tolerate.

Jo had to be with Martina.

All the time Jo was searching for her, she was hiding in one of the many cupboards where cleaning materials were kept. She knew the City would be closing. She needed to be alone. She did not want to see Jo again, neither inside the building nor outside. She would hide and stay in the City overnight. She had done it before. When things at home had got too much with her parents or her sister, she would camp out at the City overnight. It was not a problem. As soon as the security guards had locked up she would enter the staff room, where there were sofas and coffee making facilities. She could sleep there using the clean towels as blankets. She needed time to be alone. She needed time to think.

The news of Jo's departure had sent her into a frenzy of anger and distrust. She had never considered that he would leave. Suddenly his news had thrust her into a black hole. He was obviously not to be trusted. He was somebody who could hurt her. He was somebody who could destroy her equilibrium. She had to think how to manage this situation.

From being her 'perfect' partner, Jo was now relegated to being someone she had to fear. Someone who she was suddenly learning to hate. Her perfect partner was now her adversary. She needed to consider what to do about him. Also she could not understand why he had given her a passport. What was she to do with a passport in a strange name? Who was Martina Green? Everything was suddenly too confusing for her.

Her breathing got laboured. She felt pain in her head. She closed her eyes and listened; her body was screaming at her from within. For the past months she had not felt like this. All the time she had felt safe with her perfect Jo, her body had behaved. Her mind had been placid. She had not felt the fear and anger she usually felt. Now, once again she found herself experiencing her usual painful emotions.

Jo had told her he was leaving. This had triggered her usual response of realising that she would need to discard him before he could leave her. She had to win. She had to be in control. She would not let him abandon her. He was evil. He needed to be taught a lesson. She had split him. He had moved from being her perfect lover into being a demon … a demon who must be crushed … a demon who she must discard. Her Perfect King had become her Dark Demon. After lighting up a cigarette, she opened the bottle that she always kept in her rucksack. She then turned on her phone and listened to Marina Lin singing 'This is What Depression Feels Like'. Martina knew exactly what it felt like. She would always listen to Marina sing when life got too difficult. It did not stop her pain but it made Martina realise that she was not the only one in the world with problems. Others felt the same way too.

Suddenly, listening to Marina Lin singing, she was transported to considering her last discard. They had only been together for six weeks before she had to get rid of her. She had been thoughtless. She had not been around on one Saturday when Martina really wanted her, really needed her body. That was why she had discarded her. She began to consider all the other hurtful individuals she had been forced to discard. So many partners who had been transported from being perfect, into becoming dangerous beings, threatening her equilibrium.

'Stop,' Martina yelled at herself.

'Stop thinking about the past. The past has gone. Focus on what you need to do now.'

She realised that she was over thinking. She was being her usual hyper-vigilant self. Oblivion. Oblivion, that was all she needed now. She needed her supply. She reached again for her rucksack and lit another cigarette.

Jo's simple sentence sharing the fact that he would have to leave Slovakia had set up a tsunami within Martina.

Martina spent a disrupted night ensconced in the staffroom at AquaCity. She needed to decide what to do about Jo. Sadly, her mind had already decided that Jo was a potential danger to her. He had become a problem. All her thoughts now revolved around her distrust and fear of her previously perfect partner. He was no longer perfect. She needed to regain control. She needed to find a way to manage the situation.

In the past she had either just removed herself from unwanted partners or found more intrusive, yet criminal ways to get rid of them. Despite her devastated lovers reaching out to her she would just ignore them. Eventually they would go away, sinking into their own painful confusion after being so cruelly discarded. If some chose not to go away, or to be problematic she knew how to get rid of them. She could not afford to let her reputation be tainted by gossip from ex lovers. Jo was different because she immediately knew he would be a problem. She could not give him the chance of just being ignored. She knew that her adventure with Jo had to end. She was going to gain control and take the initiative. She could not afford another scandal. Her parents and her family, even her priest, had already labelled her as 'impulsive and wicked'. Her reputation was at risk. She would have to get rid of him. Jo was about to become one of Martina's many discards. Jo's fate was sealed. This King was about to be unceremoniously dethroned.

They were both now heading towards a devastating future, with ramifications that neither of them would ever have imagined possible. Our Enchantress needed to discard her fallen King. Life was about to become overwhelming for both of them.

CHAPTER NINE

IN THE CAVES

'Our personality should be impenetrable even to ourselves.'

Fernando Pessoa, *The Book of Disquiet*

Both Jo and Martina were extremely intelligent and thoughtful. They had studied their individual labels which had been thrust upon them by well meaning professionals. They were both hyper vigilant, though self serving, concerning their actions and feelings. They both believed that they understood their respective personalities and that they were forever sensitive and awake to their lives. Perhaps it may have been easier for them if they had not delved into the world of mental health. Perhaps they would have been more comfortable if they had remained in the world of impenetrable existence, where they could just live on the surface.

Following Martina abandoning him in AquaCity, Jo had a daunting sleepless night. He felt stupid. Why had he not just told Martina that he would be taking her with him? Why had he let her just walk away when he had not even finished explaining the situation? Why had he not found her? Why had he made such a mess of the whole encounter?

The answer to all his questions lay clearly in his mind. He had never had a relationship before. He had never had to negotiate differing viewpoints or understandings. He had never had to try to accept the views and emotions of others.

He had been encased within his own brittle body. He had been stuck. He did not need to bend or move in response to anyone. He had been self-contained and self-reliant. At least that was how he perceived himself in the past. He listened to 'Boys Will Cry' by Lunar Year. The song reflected what he so often felt. He knew his 'man inside' had been locked within him for too long. He was certainly making mistakes, and now he was hurting. The song was right, the fact that we hurt is a sign that we are alive.

Now it seemed his lack of emotional intelligence and knowledge of how to engage in interacting with others, had totally let him down. He had made an enormous mess of the situation. He needed to find her and explain everything. He had high hopes that his explanation would allow her to view his departure in a more positive way, especially when she knew that he was going to take her with him.

Jo's long night of discontent ended with the bells of the local church reaching out to everyone in the town. He got up and decided to go to the City straight away. He needed to find her, and he hoped she would be at work.

Indeed, Martina was at work. She had never left work. She was preparing to start her day by initially hiding in her cleaning cupboard again until her fellow workers were moving around the pools, then she would merge into the scene as if she had just joined them. No one would notice. No one would even consider that perhaps she had been there all night. She had often stayed in the City. Many nights she would not want to go home. Home could be problematic. Her parents, her sister, and even her neighbours would be critical of her. She would find the solitude and succour she needed in the City. On many occasions when she crashed overnight in the City, she would be accompanied by a new conquest. Another King or Queen, who could meet her needs for a short period. She would allow them to hide with her in the cupboard, and then they would be able to spend the night in the showers or swimming in the pools. At night AquaCity became her playground. The City allowed her freedom and escape. It was her own personal nocturnal playground.

However, tonight she did not feel like playing. Her night spent in the City had been a lonely one. Her emotions were still jangled as the sun warmed the building. Her colleagues were arriving. She stealthily moved from her cupboard towards the main pool. She had just arrived for work. No one would think anything else.

Whilst she was negotiating her day, Jo was walking towards the front entrance to the complex. The moment the building opened its doors Jo was the first to enter. He did not change into his swimming gear; instead he scoured the halls and corridors. Previously, they had never met in the mornings. They had always been together in the evenings. Martina was not expecting to see Jo. Indeed, she no longer wanted to see Jo. Jo had become a persona non grata. Jo had been removed from her mind. So, when they came eye to eye in the corridor leading to the main pool, she was shocked. Jo was delighted. He reached out to her. She recoiled. They both stood motionless, not knowing what to do next. They remained still for several seconds. Despite himself, Jo took the initiative. It was the first time he had ever taken the initiative with her. He was taking the control. The sound system began its daily toil. 'I Don't Want to Lose You' by Tina Turner bounced around the walls. Jo listened. All he could do was plead with her.

'I need you. I cannot go to Djibouti without you. You must come with me. We cannot be apart.'

Martina had heard similar words before. Similar protestations of undying love from those she had discarded. Pleas of forgiveness from those unfortunate discards who never understood what they needed to do to gain her forgiveness or even what they had done in order to need to be forgiven. They would be confused and lost, wondering why they had been so quickly and cruelly discarded.

A cold funnel of protective ice seemed to swirl around Martina's body. She realised that Jo's obvious possessiveness was going to be a problem for her. She needed to escape from his expectations, from his impending engulfment. She no longer needed him. He had become someone she feared. He could damage her. She had spent the night knowing that he had not treated her well. She knew love could disappear overnight. She had played the Beatles tune last night, just as she had played it on so many other nights when she knew that love had disappeared. 'I'm Looking Through You' played in her mind. She no longer knew Jo.

Jo could not understand her coldness. He reached out again. She turned and walked away, just as she had done the previous day. This time Jo was ready. He quickly moved towards her and grabbed her from behind, pulling her towards him and attempting to kiss her. Realising that a scene could draw attention to her, Martina quickly changed tactics. She could not let anyone know what had been going on. She could not let her colleagues realise who she was. In a flash she knew what to do. She had to placate Jo. She had to take back control. She turned and smiled. The actress in her began her perfected performance. She turned towards him, putting her hands gently on either side of his distraught face. Then she slowly kissed him, finally whispering, in her most seductive voice,

'Not here, not now. We must talk but we need to be somewhere private. I can get off. Wait for me outside and I'll join you in about ten minutes.'

Jo accepted the arrangement. She had soothed him. He turned from her towards the exit, whilst she moved purposefully towards the office. She soon found her manager, and gave the excuse that she felt a migraine coming on and that she would have to go home. This was accepted and Martina left the building. She soon found Jo by the front entrance and the two of them began walking towards the town centre. It was the first time they had been together outside the City. Little did either of them realise that this excursion was to have dramatic repercussions for them both.

The Demanovska Cave system in the Low Tatras is known worldwide. There are enormous domed ceilings and numerous pools within this large Karst complex which was discovered just over one hundred years ago. Stalagmites and stalactites adorn the corridors. The caves and pools are numerous, with the Liberty Cave and the Emerald Lake being the most spectacular features. Many Slovakians attest to the curative properties of the air within the cave system. The caves lie in the Slovak Paradise National Park, situated in eastern Slovakia. There are hiking trails with ladders, chains and bridges. It is a magical physical environment, perfect for escape and enjoyment.

A second area of exceptional national beauty is found around the Dobsinska Ice Cave. It is one of the most beautiful places in Slovakia, being one of the largest ice caves in the world. Visitors need to wrap up warm as it is very cold, usually about minus forty degrees. The ice is approximately twenty-five metres thick in some areas. There are numerous steps and walkways, which at times can be very slippery. Odd rocks and strange configurations appear from below the sheets of ice and snow. There is a distinctive smell which permeates the air. Sadly, the noise of the many visitors talking and the clatter of their boots on the metal walkways disturbs the silence of the ice crafted sculptures.

Martina had visited both cave systems many times as a child. Both caves offered her escape. She needed to escape frequently. Her parents had enjoyed hiking and had been determined to show her and her sister the beauty of their beloved country. Her father, who was Turkish, had moved to Slovakia when he was eighteen. He soon met her mother and they married only months after falling in love. For many years they were childless. Fearing they would never have children, Martina had been adopted as an infant. Several years later, Anna, her half sister had been born. Martina sometimes felt close to her mother and sister, but her father's drinking habits, and aggressive behaviour meant that she was always frightened when he was near. He had little time for the girls, and though he really wanted a son, he was reluctant to bring any more children into the family, as he recognised the expense associated with each new child. Her parents' union had gradually been emptied of love but filled with two needy growing children. Her pragmatic father knew two children would be more than enough.

Although Martina still lived in the family home, she often would stay out all night. In the past she had had many quasi relationships, always short lived. Her parents could not accept her attitude to sex. They had tried to quell her behaviour; indeed they had taken her to see many medical practitioners. She had been passed around the various doctors, psychologists and psychiatrists living in Slovakia. No one seemed to be able to help as they could not accept who she was. Her angry outbursts were frequent and alarming. She would frighten her mother who would just leave the house and head for the peace of the nearby woods, leaving Martina to calm down. At other times Martina would appear vacant, lost in a different world of her own conjuring. She would refuse to answer questions, turning herself into an elective mute. She would ignore her sister and anyone who came near. She was constantly developing lies as she mixed her immediate reality with her fantasy worlds and contorted understandings.

Her family had really given up on her. They wished she would move away. Indeed, her father had found her jobs in Bratislava, hoping she would apply and move to the city. Martina did not move from the family home. Whilst she disliked her father and was afraid of his outbursts, she felt she needed to be near her mother. Her mother seemed to put up with her, even love her. She failed to realise that her mother was living on a knife edge, thinking that Martina's anger and aggressive behaviour was just being copied from her father. Martina's mother was fearful of her husband and her daughter. She had no love for either of them. She wished she could just walk out of the door and leave her family to their own devices. She knew she would never do such a thing, but she could always dream.

Martina and Jo walked away from the constraints of AquaCity towards a new freedom. Martina was heading for the bus terminal. She had planned to take a bus to the countryside. Beauty and green surroundings would help her manage her inner turmoil. Nature, fresh air and breathing would help her know what to do. She would take Jo to either the Demanovska Caves or to the Ice Cave. Hadn't he been asking to visit the countryside with her? She would be giving him what he wanted, whilst she would find solace in her exceptional natural escapes.

They arrived at the bus terminal. She checked the departures board. The first bus was heading for The Demanovska Cave system. That would be their destination. She so loved the area, particularly the Emerald Lake. As she had visited the area many times, she knew all the walkways and shortcuts by heart. Her aunt usually worked on the reception desk at the entrance to the cave complex. Her aunt never made her pay when she visited. It would be the perfect place. Peace, quiet, solitude and overwhelming beauty. She would take Jo to see the Emerald Lake. There, she was assured that they would find both peace and tranquillity. Her favourite word, 'perfect' caressed Martina's mind again.

They bought their tickets and boarded the bus, going to the back where they could sit away from the other passengers. Martina took Jo's hand. She did not want to talk; she just wanted to keep Jo placated. She needed to draw as little attention to herself as possible. This trip was to be memorable. Fortunately, there were only about two people on the bus, and they were so engrossed in their own conversation they seemed not to notice Martina and her distraught Jo.

On arriving at the caves Martina asked Jo to wait by the toilet block while she went to the entrance booth to get tickets. Luck was on her side. She did not have to buy tickets. Her aunt reached out with a hug as Martina leant on the counter. They exchanged a few words about the family then Martina told her aunt, that she just needed to escape into the caves for her usual spiritual experience. Her aunt was very religious and knew that Martina would often visit the caves, seeking just such an experience. On discovering when the next accompanied tour would be taking place, Martina realised that there would be forty minutes of alone time that they could spend in the caves before the next tour set off. She thanked her aunt and moved away from the booth, towards the entrance gate. Jo watched her as she gesticulated for him to join her. Her aunt pressed the button which released the locked gate, and they both walked through and into the complex. Fortunately, the gate could not be seen from the booking booth. Martina's aunt had not seen them enter the caves.

Martina and Jo now owned the caves. They had the complex to themselves. The magical beauty of their surroundings was about to offer them spiritual succour. Martina knew that these caves had served her well all her life. They would allow her to breathe the special recuperative air. They would allow her to sort out all her problems. The caves nurtured her. She would soon have her life under control again.

Jo was overcome by the beauty and cold crispness of being underground. He at last was sharing the wonders of the world with his Enchantress. Despite being concerned as to their future together, Jo knew that this move from the City towards the beauty of the caves was the next stage in their relationship. This was the beginning of their new life together. They were out in the world, side by side. If Martina could leave the City and join him on a bus towards the caves, she would be able to board a plane by his side and travel to Djibouti with him. He would soon have his life with her back on track again.

The narrow pathway was dangerous. They held onto the handrail whilst their feet negotiated the icy stone as they descended into the semi-darkness. Together, they walked carefully down the slippery slope of their future, both feeling that they would soon have everything back in control.

The cave system was indeed magnificent. Stalagmites and stalactites adorned the surroundings. The glistening transparency of the icy rocks shivered with startling silver brightness as the strategically placed electric lights illuminated their hidden wonders. What nature had created, man had enhanced. The place was surely a spiritual escape. A wonder of our world. A place where everything was possible. Martina sighed. The air was helping her heal her inner wounds. The air would nourish her. She would be whole again. She would not be fearful. The air would tell her how to deal with this man walking beside her. Her spiritual world would be regained. All would be well. They moved together along the narrow pathways which twisted around the cavernous corners of the complex. They arrived at the large cave which held the Emerald Lake. From the walkway it was about ten metres of stony cliffside down into the waters. The cliff was not entirely vertical, but staggered and punctuated by numerous stalagmites and indentations. Martina told Jo that this was her favourite part of the caves.

'Look deep into my Emerald Lake,' she encouraged him. 'The Lake is magical. The Lake always solves my problems.'

Holding hands, they moved along the walkway. Martina stopped walking, telling Jo that this was the best viewpoint and that if he just leant forward and peered into the emerald waters he would appreciate the magic of the lake. Jo did as she suggested. He looked down. The lake seemed a long way off, yet he could see the luminosity of the green emerald waters. Like Martina, he appreciated its beauty. He hoped that the lake would be as generous to him as it had been to her. He wanted all his problems to be solved too.

On some level, they both knew instinctively that, for them, everything was about to change. The lake would offer them both the salvation they yearned.

Thirty minutes later, Martina left the cave networks alone. She was smiling and sighing gently. She felt the sun on her face as she looked towards the knowing sky. The universe was on her side. Her spiritual world had once again, supported her. She had visited her favourite lake, the Emerald Lake. Indeed, the lake had offered a simple resolution to all her problems. The lake had endorsed the ideas the air had suggested to her. It had enticed her towards a simple action which solved all her concerns. She had only to give a gentle push as she and Jo peered into the green glassed oblivion below them.

Then it was done. For a short time, the lake's perpetual stillness had been disturbed, absorbing all her problems. Jo was now surrounded by his favourite colour. The emerald green waters had enveloped him and his fractured skull. He lay submerged and motionless in his icy tomb. Some moments later, the stillness returned to the lakes surface and with it, Martina's equilibrium. All the obstacles to her life had simply disappeared below the surface of her Emerald Lake. Martina would be safe.

She left the complex. She was lighter, she was soothed, and she was herself again. She closed the gate behind her and returned to the booth, thanking her aunt and saying that her life would be well from now on. She had had her spiritual fix. She hugged her aunt and turned to leave.

'Wait a moment,' called her aunt, 'haven't you forgotten something?'

Martina went cold. She froze around the words. Her thoughts piled on top of each other, each one groping for supremacy. How did her aunt know? How could her aunt have seen Jo enter the complex with her? How would she explain him not being here now? As well as a multitude of questions, her exemplary mind concocted an array of acceptable explanations. Of course, it had just been an accident. She had had nothing to do with it. He had just over-reached and fallen into the emerald waters. The contortions of her jumbled mind threw a dark confusion across her eyes.

'You don't realise what has happened, do you?' interjected her aunt, wondering at Martina's obvious distress. 'When you were here earlier your glasses were perched on the top of your head ... Now they have gone.'

Martina put her hand to her head, yes, her glasses had gone. From being overwhelmed she now became relieved.

Her actress found her slick cue again, 'Oh I'm always losing them. No problem, they are very cheap and I have another pair at home. I love green glasses, they are my signature.'

The clever part of Martina thought that she might not be able to wear green glasses again. She soon pushed this thought away. She had another pair. She would use her second pair, and then when they had worn out she pondered what she could do. She quickly made a decision. She would paint her nails green. That would be her signature in future.

'Yes,' she said to herself, 'and maybe green toe nails too, that would be distinctive.'

Even after her so called spiritual existence in the cave she was still able to consider issues of fashion and ways to enhance her body. She was a remarkable individual.

Natalie Cole singing 'Smile 'came from the speakers surrounding the building as a coach load of visitors carefully walked towards the gift shop and toilet block. Martina's mind tried to remain calm, to placate her emotions and justify the actions she had been forced to carry out in the caves. She knew that her psyche would always be tainted. She knew that some things cannot be forgotten. Despite always obsessively cleansing her outward self, Martina knew her inward self was intractably soiled. Some things certainly were unforgettable. For those things there would never be any forgiveness.

She hugged her aunt again and headed for the bus stop. Soon she would be home. All would be well. She took Natalie's advice from the song and tried to smile. Life would be worthwhile if she could just smile. Her fake smile quivered on her face as the bus navigated numerous potholes on its way towards Poprad. Her escape had begun.

CHAPTER TEN

ESCAPE

'Distance means so little when someone means so much.'

JM Barrie, *Peter Pan*

After hugging and leaving her aunt sitting in her kiosk, Martina boarded the waiting bus. She was leaving the caves and heading back to Poprad. She needed to put as much distance between herself and her actions as she could. Perhaps if she could get far enough away she would be able to forget what had happened. In the past she had always been able to remove herself from any trauma. Nothing seemed to affect her. She would remove herself and forget. Somehow she felt that she might not be able to forget Jo. She knew on some deep level that Jo was different, but she could always hope. Hope to forget. She could not allow her mind to be contaminated by her past deeds. She decided that she would indeed forget.

She put her earplugs in and listened to Beth Crowley singing 'Perfect Doesn't Last'. The song helped her to recognise that there were others just like her, others who had been let down. She was not the only one. She needed perfection, yet she knew perfection never lasted. Her partners were never enough. Everyone was flawed.

When the song had finished, she knew what she would have to do. Her survival-focused self knew what her next course of action would have to be. On reaching Poprad's bus station and leaving the bus, she headed towards the small travel agent shop next to the supermarket. She needed to quit the country. She needed to leave as soon as possible. She smiled at the young man who greeted her, she knew him. After polite 'how are yous', she asked if he could organise a flight to London by the end of the week. A one-way ticket was booked. Martina would leave Slovakia. London would offer new opportunities, but most of all it would put space between her and her actions.

Martina needed to distance herself from everything she had previously known. She was to begin again. She was to be a new woman. She would leave everything behind. All those 'knowing' individuals who had tried to label her condition, all those discards who had pretended to love her, all her workmates who had argued with her or been disrespectful. But most of all, the main thing she wanted to leave behind was her family. She knew her mother might miss her, but she was delighted to think that there was no need to ever see her father or her sister again … ever again. Her life in London would be perfect.

Returning home, she broke the news to her amazed parents. She was going to leave Slovakia. They knew by her demeanour that she was determined to leave. They would not be able to get her to change her decision. On some level, they did not want her to change her decision. She had been a cause of much concern to them and to the distant family and friends. She was not predictable. She had a temper. Despite going to two anger management courses she was still violent at times. Her behaviour was usually strange at best and inappropriate at least. She had left the school, where she had previously taught, under a cloud. Her parents had been happy to see that she was able to get work at AquaCity, though soon rumours and gossip began to start again. Why could she not be just like her sister? Why did she always behave strangely? Her parents smiled knowingly at each other. They would be happy to see her leave Slovakia. She was a problem to them. She should go elsewhere. Anywhere else.

Following breaking her news, Martina went to her room and began sorting out the things she would need to take with her. She found her spare green glasses alongside her medication in her bedside cabinet and put them in her rucksack. Tired, she lay on her bed. The day in the caves had been exhausting. So much had happened. So much had demanded her control. She had needed to interpret and understand all the messages she had been given. She had needed to follow her internal instructions. She had worked well. The day had been a success.

London, the word exploded out of her head, cascaded over her shoulders and travelled through her body. London would be a happy escape. On telling her parents that she was leaving she had not told them where she was going. Sheer distaste entered her mouth. They had not even asked where she was going. She realised that they did not care. All they cared about was the fact that she was leaving.

Martina swallowed then quickly ran to the bathroom. She was violently sick. Bile joined with her distaste and disappeared into the porcelain bowl. She flushed them away. Soon she would flush her family away too. She was good at flushing. Water would help her. Water would cleanse her. She had a vague remembrance … hadn't the water in the Emerald Lake already solved all her problems?

Sitting on her bed she began to compose a letter to her boss. She apologised for having to leave work because of the onset of a migraine. She explained that as she often suffered from visual migraines, it was best if she relinquished her position. She did not want to risk letting the City down. Finally, she requested that he email a reference to her, based on the work she had already undertaken. She left the house and walked to the post box, feeling relieved that she was back in control again. She was managing her life. Soon all her past problems and people would be forgotten. Her new life was about to start. Martina would be victorious.

Her boss was quite relieved to receive her resignation. He had become aware of her questionable behaviour at the City. People were beginning to talk. He did not want any trouble. She may have helped fix some of the equipment but he had always felt she would be difficult. He knew she had a temper for he had heard her argue with many of the other trainers. She was not liked. He put her letter in the bin and ignored her request for a reference. He was well rid or her.

Her parents had unwittingly named her well. Martina meant 'servant of Mars 'or 'Enchantress of war'. She knew how to fight. She knew how to win. She would always protect herself. She caressed the tattoo on her wrist which covered one of her self-harming attempts. The thunderbolt tattoo reassured her. She was indeed a true Martina.

The end of the week found our victorious Enchantress sitting in a cramped room in a small hotel opposite St Pancras Station. There was no window but at least it was cheap. She was scouring the local London ads on her phone, looking for any jobs which she might be able to manage. Her English was good. She was bright. She had a master's degree in business studies, but she knew that such a degree would not be much help in the frenetic world of London businesses. She needed to find a job which would not challenge her too much, but which would allow her to function and be comfortable. A job which granted her access to people and a structured timetable. Time management was important. But most of all, the surroundings needed to be super clean. Cleanliness was one of her major requirements. Water and showers were an absolute necessity.

Realising that she now would have to be completely self-reliant, she began to worry. Would she have enough money? Living with her parents for so many years meant that she had never had to be concerned about money. She realised that now she needed another sort of supply. Not only did she need sex but now she needed money. She posted on her feed, 'All I need people for is the supply of money or sex.'

There was an advert for a trainer at a London gym.

'That would be perfect,' she said to the mirror on the wall.

Picking up her phone, she rang the gym. Amazingly, after a short interchange the manager who answered her call pleaded,

'Come now, we really are in a difficult position. Two of our trainers are unwell and we cannot cover their classes.'

So that was how Martina began her work in London.

Back in Slovakia things were not so perfect. Several days after she had visited the caves, one of the more observant tour guides had seen a strange object glinting on the icy bank, just above the water line of the Emerald Lake. It looked like glass but it was difficult to see because it was a long way down to the lake. The terrain was dangerous. He was about to get a rope ladder to try to climb down to remove the offending object when he realised that the stalagmites on either side of the route he intended to take had been broken. His mind went into overdrive. Who had broken them? No one was allowed to leave the designated route. No one ever climbed over the wet rock faces. How had the rocks been disturbed, and the stalagmites broken? Had someone left the pathway? What was the object? He decided to do nothing. He would just tell his boss.

His boss was called and soon they were both looking towards the glinting light of the mysterious object. They could not understand why the stalagmites between the pathway and the lake had been broken. There was something which was not quite right. After several discussions with the other men who worked at the caves, it was decided that it would be too dangerous for anyone to try to climb down towards the lake. They could not retrieve the object that way. However, there was a small bank the other side of the lake which was accessible. They could launch their portable coracle from there and row across the waters to where the offending object had been seen. The coracle was duly fetched, and the lightest guide took the paddle and pointed the boat in the direction of the green object. The others all looked on from the safety of the fenced pathway, high above the water.

After much splashing and jovial encouragement from his work colleagues, he eventually reached the side of the lake which held the offending object. He was close enough to see that it was a pair of green glasses. Martina's unwittingly discarded green glasses glinted in the torch light. He used his paddle to scrape the glasses from the rocky bank towards the lake waters, and then he hooked them onto his oar and carefully balanced them towards the boat. Eureka ... he had them. Everyone clapped. He then returned the paddle to the water and began turning the boat around in order to cross the lake again. The paddle knocked against something bulky between the boat and the lake's edge. He had hit something.

Further investigation introduced him to our dear schizoid friend. He had found Jo. He shouted to the other guides, telling them.

'It's a body. There's a body in the shallow water at the edge. There's a dead body in the lake.'

The chatter and laughter from the walkway above stopped. Everyone looked on in disbelief. There were a few seconds of silence then someone started to laugh, either through nervousness or perhaps thinking it was joke. There could not be a body in the water. Every visitor was accompanied by a guide. Everyone had been accounted for. All visitors were counted on entering and leaving the caves. It could not be a body. The main guide shouted.

'Come back. Bring the glasses but don't touch anything else.'

Some forty minutes later the police arrived at the caves. Ropes were dispatched, boats launched, and instructions given on how to remove the body from its emerald green tomb. The police were efficient and careful. Jo was removed from the water and returned to dry land.

The investigation began. All staff members were questioned again and again. No one could understand how it could have happened. They had strict protocols at the caves. Every person entering had to be accompanied. Every person, on entering and on leaving had to be counted. No one could enter the caves without a guide. It was a simple straightforward safety process that had worked well for years.

Martina's aunt observed all the activity. She listened to all the explanations as to how it could not have happened. She recognised Martina's glasses but decided not to mention the fact that she had let Martina enter the caves on her own. Jobs were difficult to come by. She did not want to lose her job. Martina had told her that she had another pair of glasses. What would be the point of saying that she knew who the glasses belong to? Martina could have had nothing to do with the man in the lake. Martina had gone into the caves for her spiritual meditation. She had been alone. It had been an innocent visit. Well mainly innocent. Perhaps not making Martina buy a ticket was not so innocent. Perhaps that was indirect theft but as it was just a simple senseless act of nepotism, she could ignore it. No, her decision was made. She would not say anything. She would forget the whole affair. That way she would not even have to mention it to her priest at her next confession. It had never happened.

The police placed Jo in a dark green body bag which they then carried to the awaiting ambulance. He was taken to the nearest morgue. His body and his clothes were examined. It was agreed that he had not been in the water long. It looked as though a skull fracture had been the cause of death, most probably as he fell towards the lake. There was very little on the body which could help them identify him, only a key with a plastic label attached and a strange large black bead on a ribbon. On the key label was the number three.

The following day, one of the more able detectives tracked down where the key had been issued. He had checked all the estate agents in the area. One of them recognised the plastic label. It was a label her company would use for all their rental properties. It was not long before they accepted that the key did belong to Jo, and they then gave the detective the address of the property he had been renting. Jo had previously given the estate agent a false name, but the police were happy to accept it.

A promising result. The police were delighted to be interviewed for the local paper, telling the reporters that only twenty-four hours after discovery of the body they had been able to identify the man in question and had also discovered where he lived. A very positive outcome. The police, the reporters and eventually all those reading the article were delighted to recognise such proficient police work. Their delight was doubled, on realising that the body was not a local man. No need to worry about close relatives or friends who lived nearby. The body belonged to a stranger.

The police had known that he was not a local man following a visit to his flat. The key turned easily in the lock. They entered a stale but tidy flat. Some money sat in a file on the mantelpiece. He had few possessions and what little food had been kept in his fridge was still within its sell by date. He had not been gone long. They found no phone or computer. Nothing which would help them to identify who he was. Jo had secreted all important items in a locking fireproof box, which he had buried in the overgrown garden to the rear. When Jo had initially buried it he had smiled to himself, thinking that despite all the modern technology, the best ploys were those which had been used for years. Jo was used to keeping things hidden.

However, Jo had not concealed his make-up. The shelves in his small bathroom were adorned with all sorts of good quality creams, astringents and serums. Numerous lipsticks, eye shadows and mascaras jostled for supremacy in a large woven basket. In contrast to the jumble of items in the basket, his array of perfumes stood upright to attention. Six erect glass bottles, promising the olfactory delights of various fragrances adorned the space at the head of the bath. The police looked at each other with confusion. They had been told that the flat was inhabited by only one man. Now it looked as if a woman was residing there too.

The police continued with their investigations. They were happy with how the case was developing. They were proving to themselves and to the public that they were efficient and competent. A police force to be reckoned with.

Three days after the discovery of Jo's body and numerous visits to his flat, the two main detectives leading the case were summoned into the boss's office. Here they were told that they were being relieved of the case and would they please not mention any of their findings or observations to anyone else. They were to be quiet. Everything had to be hush-hush. The case had been moved upstairs. They were to have no more involvement. This they reluctantly did. Orders are orders. There were no more interviews and the case appeared to have been officially closed. As far as the local police were concerned, Jo and their investigation had to be forgotten.

However, during discussions in Bratislava's police head-quarters, Jo's dilemma was far from forgotten. The situation became daily more strained. Differing viewpoints and polit-ical considerations meant that there was much confusion regarding the body which had been found in the caves.

The local police dealt with the situation well, but obvi-ously did not have the resources to undertake further inves-tigations. Detectives were sent first from Trencin and then from Bratislava. It had initially seemed to be a simple open and shut case. The man had obviously died due to a fall and a blow to the skull. However, there appeared to be many questions still not answered. How had the accident hap-pened? How did the man enter the caves? How long had he been there? Also, there was still much perplexity regarding who had been living with him at the flat. The make-up had thrown a red herring into the Slovakian bouillabaisse.

Who was the woman sharing the flat with Jo? Where was she now?

Though no one was actually saying anything, there did seem to be some concern over the status of the deceased. He was not just an ordinary tourist. This man from the Emerald Lake held many secrets, not least why he was living in Slovakia and what work he was undertaking. There were too many concerns to allow the case to remain with the local police. Senior, experienced detectives were needed.

The detectives arriving from Bratislava seemed unapproachable. They shared few smiles and even less conversation. The gravity of secrecy permeated the police station. The euphoria of the local police at discovering, reclaiming and identifying the body, all within a short space of time, was replaced by a cold constricted cheerlessness. The new detectives caused the friendly local police offices to become almost as frozen as the caves themselves.

Detectives from Bratislava were important. They had national work to do. They were aloof. Even offers of hot cups of tea or coffee were initially refused as the detectives set up their temporary workstations. They were aware of the importance of this random body which had died so unceremoniously within their borders. They had received notification from Head Office that the case could prove to be of international importance and that they were to ensure that they gave the investigation their fullest attention.

Gradually as the local police absorbed the gravitas of the situation, they talked less about their obvious abilities at finding Jo and began to look towards supporting their superior colleagues. Despite being taken off the case they were still eager to discover who the fractured skull belonged to and what was he doing in Poprad. The atmosphere had changed.

Everyone was attempting to move the enquiry onto a firmer footing. Everyone wanted to know who this man had been and who was the woman sharing the flat with him.

Days of boring basic police work followed. Metod was one of the lead investigators sent from Bratislava. Metod was bright and had previously worked on many international investigations. Ironically, his name reflected his approach to his work. Metod meant 'method' and indeed he was a very able and methodological investigator. He spoke both Slovakian and English. He had studied in England for three years as a student and had perfect diction. His ear was good and he could even emulate different accents. He would make his family laugh as he changed from Scottish to Welsh to Irish in one sentence.

As the investigation progressed there seemed little to discover. The breakthrough came when quite by chance; a Ukrainian arrived at the flat looking for Jo. It seemed that this innocent Ukrainian would meet Jo for tea every other Wednesday at four pm in the tea shop. His job was to either give packages to Jo or take items from Jo, which he then returned to Ukraine. He never knew Jo's name. On first meeting he had been told to go to the tea house and look for the man in an orange shirt with orange loafers, and just give him the package. He explained that he had nothing to do with the packages. They were just left in a plastic bag behind his plant trough which sat outside his house in Lviv. He never saw anyone deliver or collect the packages. Money for payment and expenses was put in an envelope and placed though his letter box. It was a simple job that was well paid.

But today Jo had not turned up for their usual meeting. Our Ukrainian mule guessed that Jo lived above the tea shop. During one meeting Jo had forgotten something and had to return to his flat to collect it. He had been gone only a few minutes, so his flat had to be near, and as he had not left the building, our clever mule had deduced that the flat had to be above the shop.

He explained to the police why he was there today. It was Wednesday. It was four o'clock. He was due to meet Jo as usual. Jo had not turned up so, as he had a package for delivery, he decided to leave the tea rooms and go to the flat to seek Jo. That was how he found himself drawn into the police investigation.

The lead detective took the package from him. The detectives, Metod, the Ukrainian and the package returned to the police station. After several hours of extensive questioning interspersed with long periods of intimidatory silence, they allowed our mule to return to his home in Ukraine. They believed he had little more to give them. They did not have the jurisdiction to move their enquiries across the border into Ukraine. Things were volatile. The only real lead they had was the package.

Everyone's attention focused on the package. Metod cautiously opened the small brown parcel. Inside was a plain white envelope addressed to Peter Pan.

It was a letter.

My Dear Peter Pan,

It is good to hear from you after so long. No, I have not forgotten you. I will never forget you. I was touched to receive your letter and to acknowledge that you chose me as the only person you could reach out to. Thank you so much for realising that you could share so much with me. I am heartened to know that after all this time, you still trust me.

Yes, I do know how you feel about meeting your soul mate. That was how I felt when I met you, but I suppose we all must experience unrequited love at one time or another. Thank you for so generously apologising for your behaviour in Hawaii. I should have realised that you were not of my persuasion. I too must apologise for my actions that night.

SO, AT LAST, WE HAVE BOTH APOLOGISED AND HOPE-FULLY FORGIVEN EACH OTHER!

But now you tell me you are truly 'in love'. She sounds intriguing. I have never met a Green Enchantress, or even a green god! I do hope all goes well for you. We all need closeness and intimacy in our lives. Both you and I know how difficult it is to find the right 'match' for our desires, hopes and expectations.

I agree that some of her behaviours you describe do sound perplexing. But then many people behave strangely, that does not mean you can't love them. Sometimes the very 'strangeness' becomes part of the attraction. There are so many interpretations of sexual fulfilment and of gender enjambment. We cannot hope to understand them all, only to accept them.

We, as humans are evolving all the time. I expect that one day humans will be in a position of accepting the many different bodies, personalities, orientations, and minds that emerge. Sadly, we have a long way to go yet. But for today, I am glad that you feel you have found your twin flame. Let it not matter what the world thinks.

You ask me for advice. I am not competent to offer advice in this area. I know little of relationships in general and even less of intimate or sexual relationships. All I can say is try to always be completely honest and true to yourself. Listen to Emeli Sandé singing 'Read All About It'. We, none of us must continue to hide. Our differences make us all wonderfully unique. Let's all sing!

Good Luck

Let me know how things progress.

From

Mark aka your Lost Boy

PS 1) Knowing about the volatile situation at the moment I have sent this via the Government Intelligence Agency network, which I know can sometimes take time. I hope it finds its way to you – eventually!

2) I still have one big regret. Sorry we did not go to Diamond Head to find the green sand/pixie dust! Forgive me.

The detectives looked at each other. This was a personal letter. They had not expected anything of this ilk. Their enquiries had focused on Jo's work between Slovakia and Ukraine. They had suspected that he was working for the British Government. They knew the situation was delicate. They had wondered if his death had been anything to do with his role, effectively his role as a spy. So how did this letter fit into the picture? Why was a personal letter being sent via the Government Intelligence Agency? Who was this Lost Boy called Mark? Indeed, who was Peter Pan? Was the letter in code? Was it about the woman who had been sharing the flat with Jo? Where was Diamond Head?

Things were getting even more befuddled regarding the body which had been found in the caves. Things were not as clear cut as had initially been thought. Finally, the local police and the detectives from Bratislava were brought together within a shared understanding. A shared understanding they found uncomfortable. They were all totally confused. Cognitive dissonance ruled.

Metod knew it was time for him to leave Slovakia and visit his English colleagues. Perhaps then he would be able to answer some of the questions which surrounded this man called Jo or Peter Pan. He picked up the phone and spoke to his immediate boss. It was soon agreed that he should leave for England. The next day saw Metod sitting in the business class section of a plane heading from Bratislava to London.

Metod had been sent to look for the Lost Boy called Mark.

CHAPTER ELEVEN

MYSTIFYING MINDSETS

'Ah, it's my longing for whom I might have been that distracts and torments me.'

Fernando Pessoa, *The Book of Disquiet*

The time in the caves had certainly changed their worlds. But let's try to unpick their last time together in AquaCity. Their internal longings caused them to be both distracted and tormented. What had been happening to them?

The music travelling round AquaCity was well chosen. Sigrid was singing 'Bring Me the Horizon – Bad Life'. Martina felt the song resonated with her life. Now she felt it was both her and Jo singing the song. They both had the world on their shoulders and they were certainly having a bad day.

Martina and Jo had become uncomfortable. Uncomfortable with each other and with themselves. They were both aware of how they needed to manage their lives. How at a deep level they wanted, even needed, to be someone else. They both strove to move their self concepts into a demanding state of being able to live as their idealised selves. Subsequently they were forced to share a contorted and amorphous reality. It was devastating for them. They felt they did not want to be who they were. They wanted to be someone else, though neither of them knew how to start becoming another.

There were many layers to the relationship they shared. Many different interpretations of what they were experiencing. Some were superficial but others were concealed well below the surface. Their mindsets were not set, they would change and reconfigure. Everything could be moved into a new narrative. Martina could change from being ecstatic one moment to being overcome by anger the next. Their mindsets were far from being set.

So, let's try to work out what was really taking place …

Following their initial meeting at AquaCity both Jo and Martina met regularly. Their mutual love bombing created emotional explosions in their respective worlds. They had never met anyone like each other before. They seemed to fit together. They seemed to know each other's needs and be able to fulfil them without even thinking.

On a physical level they were admired by those around them, however, their close-knit companionship meant no one else was allowed to enter the world they were creating. They spent time together but neither of them needed nor wanted anyone else to invade their reveries. They were all that was required in their carefully crafted shared fantasies. They would meet most evenings at AquaCity. They would swim and work out together. Every meeting would end with fun in the showers and total exhaustion as they met and fulfilled each other's sexual needs. Although they had become enmeshed in each other's fluctuating realities they would often reflect on what was happening to them. Neither of them had ever experienced anything like it before. They were both entrapped within each other, neither wanting nor needing to leave. They had found the perfect partner. Or had they?

Just before Jo told Martina that he would be leaving for Djibouti, she lay in her bed one morning, wondering about her new 'King'. She always used superlative terms when engaging in a new relationship. Kings for men and Queens for women. So by adopting the titles 'Kings' and 'Queens' she could avoid the confusion of using real names. By always using the same titles she would not get confused when she changed partners, and she frequently changed partners.

Music would help her to manage her world. Music would calm her. She listened to the radio and the voice of Noelle Johnson singing 'Broken'. Martina's thoughts travelled round her head as she tried to calm herself. Her inner dialogue helped her affirm her beliefs. She continued her self soothing …

'Noelle's voice seems to know about me, even though she is so far away. She really understands. Sometimes I feel so broken and lost. So lonely. I need and want another. I cannot exist on my own. I feel I have nothing within. Jo seems to find me. He seems to understand me. I have never had such a long period of love bombing. It all seems real at last. It is perfect. He will never abandon me. I need have no fear of losing him. He loves me. He is obsessed with me. I feel safe and in control. Nothing can come between us. There is no jealousy because he neither wants nor needs anybody else. He is a loner. Before I invaded his world, he had no one. Before I opened him to the joys of sex, he was incomplete. I have fulfilled him. I have allowed him to feel. I have opened a world of ecstasy for him. He will never want to lose me. I will never feel abandoned.'

Martina's narcissistic viewpoint continued.

'I am in control. He will never be in a position to overwhelm me. He will never take me over. I will never be engulfed within him. I will always have the ultimate control. He cannot steal me. He cannot pull me away from myself. I am omnipotent. I am the master. I decide upon the game plan. I orchestrate all the manoeuvres. All will be well.'

Martina's new internal understandings of her needs and her own expectations, could be met by this strange new man she had targeted. Initially she had only been attracted to his body. He was beautiful. She wanted him. She needed him sexually. He could supply her sexual needs. But after finding him and discovering his aloof non-conformist approach to her seduction, she had become enthralled.

She had seen his mind and his unique way of being. She wanted to possess not just his body, but his mind as well. No one before him had ever intrigued her as much. She at last felt she may well be finding someone who was like her. At last, she had found someone who she felt she would not have to discard. Someone who would not abandon her, or leave her to manage her own confused world of unfulfilled relationships.

Martina thought that perhaps she was in love. She would prove to her parents, her sister and the doctors who had so cruelly labelled her. She would prove that people like her could maintain relationships and fall in love, just like any-body else. She listened to Westlife singing 'Alone Together'. She knew she and Jo could be alone together. It would work.

Martina was bright. Exceptionally bright. She knew what she needed and she knew how to get it. People or marks could supply what she wanted. She would target individuals and obtain exactly what she needed. She would consciously consider how to manage her marks. She had to plan her course of action carefully and with precise objectives. First she would try to show her mark how alike and compatible they both were. During the initial love bombing she would convince her target that they were soul mates. This initial period would settle into a romantic wonderment. She would try to isolate her mark from family and friends, knowing that they wanted to spend time with her and only her. Her new mate would think that they had found true love. They would trust and rely upon her. They would feel they had known her all their life, almost like a déjà vu experience. They would become detached from their own reality, living in the magical world she promised.

Then she would gradually introduce tactics to make them feel insecure. She would lie and twist her words to confuse them. She would pull them to her then not be available, making them feel insecure. They would start to question their own reality. They would begin not trusting their perceptions and understandings. They would become unstable. Then Martina could begin to take control. Her world and her reality would surround and confused them. Music and rhythms would help to co-ordinate their brain waves as the discombobulated mates accepted her strange fantasy. It would be as if they were intoxicated or disillusioned, a sort of madness. Martina would pull her targets into her world. She would want them so long as they could supply what she needed. It could be sex, drugs, money, or praise; whatever she needed at the time. However, if they failed to be able to supply what she needed she would then discard them. They would no longer be of use to her. She would move onto her next mark. Sometimes she would just move on because she was bored, or irritated by them. It was all very contrived and controlling.

Sadly the poor discarded marks would be left, lost in the distorted fantasy, unable to return to their own world and reality. Their minds would have been contaminated. They would be lost, longing for her return. They would remember all the good times but by some strange psychological distortion they would fail to consider the bad times. Consequently they would long for her and the fantasy she had created. Her production would be complete, but she would have left the stage and moved onto a new drama.

With Jo it had been different. He was already in his own strange solitary world. She did not need to try to isolate him from others. She did not have to consciously try to control him. He was ripe for picking. The sex had been the deciding factor with Jo. The sex had ensured that he needed to be with her. She transformed him into this new way of living and wanting. She managed to permeate his fortified exterior and seep into his previously unknown consciousness.

As Martina was considering her relationship with Jo, so Jo was pondering his world. How had he become entangled within the beautiful Siren with the Green Glasses? Why was he now obsessed with her, always wanting to see her and listen to the music they shared whilst working out or swimming? He knew he neither needed nor wanted any other individual. He only wanted his siren.

Jo contemplated what had happened to him as he wrote in his diary ...

'I was within my own world. I neither needed nor wanted anyone else. People were just superfluous to my existence. They really did not affect me unless they tried to get close to me. Then, I could just ignore them. I could do everything on my own. I was all I needed.

My security was challenged the moment she found me in the shower and unlocked my previously closed understandings. By physically exploring me and forcing her way into my private world she created fissures and wounds. These fissures and wounds made my exterior vulnerable. Not just vulnerable in relation to letting things IN but also by allowing me to spill OUT. I was no longer in control of myself. She seemed to have opened me to another way of being, but a way of being that was under her control. She knew what she was doing. She enjoyed the control. By taking the control she could relax herself. She knew I would not leave her. I would never abandon her. I was obsessed with her. She was safe in the knowledge that I would stay with her.

We had days of loving in a close idealised wonderment. We became almost like one. We bonded, we played, we did everything to please each other and ourselves. We were one. She had control and I was compliant. It worked.'

Jo stopped writing. It was all becoming too demanding for him. He closed his mind. His seduction had been all encompassing. His seduction had changed his understanding of himself and his world. He now needed another being. Was this what being in love felt like? Jo had never expected to experience being in love. Now he felt that perhaps he was. Jo now loved his Enchantress with the Green Glasses.

So, what went wrong? At a deep level both Jo and Martina knew that their perfect existence could not last. Even before Jo told her that he was being transferred to Djibouti their world had begun to show small fissures of fear, cracks of concern, tremors of trepidation.

Such an idealised existence could not last for long. Gradually life invaded their fortress. Floods took over their lands.

They were lost within a labyrinth of ever advancing reality. This reality crept towards them daily, squeezing perfection into a small central island awaiting complete annihilation. They both felt apprehension. They both knew what was happening, though they would not admit it, either to themselves or to each other.

Martina saw her control being eroded daily. She felt that her omnipotence was being attacked. She needed to be in charge whilst at the same time she knew her position was being challenged. She was competitive. Now she was competing against Jo. She did not want to be his equal. She feared being engulfed, almost as much as she feared being abandoned by him.

Their life was becoming ritualistic. They were starting to disagree openly. They needed to spend time apart. Ironically the more Jo tried to spend time away from her, the more she became clingy and suffocating. The more she tried to pull him to her, the more Jo needed to pull away. This she saw as negation. A form of total frustration.

At the same time, she was beginning to withhold sex. She seemed to be using sex as a tool to manipulate him, to try to hold onto him. Jo felt lost. He did not know how to help her regain her control. He feared she was looking elsewhere. Jo was no longer the centre of her universe. She needed fresh supply. He worried that the sex was becoming repetitive. That it had the potential to become mundane and boring. Their idealised world was no longer ideal. A gapping fissure had cracked open between them, and they both knew they needed to flee its proximity or risk falling into its unfathomable depths.

Neuroses and insecurities set in to support Martina's brittle personality. She became fearful and frightened. Her anxieties exploded, shattering her fragile existence. She could not cope. She needed to protect herself. She also feared that her colleagues would become aware of what was going on between her and Jo. She did not want any more scandals in her life. She had already had too many problems which had been recognised by her family and her community. She could not afford any more mistakes.

Her unconscious self-protection barriers screamed into renewed life. She had not needed them for the previous months. They had been dormant. Now they were primed and ready for use. Taught and tight, her inner missiles prepared for action. Now they became most of her being. Now they could render her as a potential nuclear weapon ready for the obliteration of anything that ventured to threaten her fragile personality. She was preparing preemptive strikes and strategies in order to meet both imagined and real threats.

She was ready and sadly Jo knew that he would be her main target. He began to feel fearful. Fearful of the fact that he was being taken over by her grandiosity. She was going to excel; she was going to protect her magnificent being. Jo acknowledged that he would be left as the dismal discarded detritus. He feared he would have nowhere to hide. He felt he would be unable to return to the safety of his solitary existence, as he knew he now needed another in his life. He needed her. She was now an integral part of him. He could not be without her. Jo was totally disorientated.

So, you see, at an unconscious level things were already beginning to unravel and fall apart between our King and his Green Enchantress, though neither of them wanted to accept the fact. Perfection was being replaced. Imperfections punctuated the fabric of their lives. Soon everything was heading towards implosion. It was inevitable that it would all collide within the glorious grandeur of the Slovakian caves.

Just before leaving AquaCity Martina had listened to Joy Division's 'She's Lost Control'. The words screamed from the music system. Martina knew her inner distractions and torments would force her to eventually move into her default mode … she would lose control.

CHAPTER TWELVE

BACK IN CHELTENHAM

'When you wake in the morning, the naughtiness and evil passions with which you went to bed have been folded up small and placed in the bottom of your mind and on the top, beautifully aired, are spread out your prettier thoughts, ready for you to put on.'

JM Barrie, *Peter Pan*

Back in Cheltenham, Sonia had spent many nights sleeping perfectly since Mark's death. Mark's suicide was over. Things seemed to have settled down. Since she had decided not to get involved with anything or anyone to do with Mark, her life seemed to return to its boring normality. On awakening each morning she was determined to only put on her 'prettier thoughts'.

Following Mark's death, she had decided to let the house as a whole property, rather than sell it. It would be far easier to manage her life if she used a local agency and just let them take over the running of the house. Before she could do this, the building needed total refurbishment. She enjoyed decorating and making a house look beautiful. Interior design was something Sonia wished she had developed professionally.

Eventually, after many setbacks due to the problem of not being able to get materials, the house was finished and looking spick and span. All the builder's merchants were having problems obtaining many of the building materials necessary for refurbishment. No one was sure why. Rumours were bouncing around between the white vans and the lorries coming from the continent. Various reasons were offered. It was because of paucity of supply. It was because of Brexit. It was because of a lack of lorry drivers. It was because incorrect orders had been proffered. No one seemed to know. Whatever the cause, the lack of materials meant that Sonia's house improvements took a very long time to accomplish.

Fortunately, Sonia had a wonderful builder. He had done a variety of work for her over the years. He was first rate, not only as a builder but also as a father, a husband and a dog owner. He was trustworthy and reliable. Everybody liked him. Sonia considered herself very fortunate to know him. Indeed, she now considered him more of a friend than a builder. As if by magic he would source materials sooner than anyone else. He was a resourceful magician of the Cheltenham construction industry. Consequently Sonia's refurbishment did not take quite as long as most other projects.

Now, at last, the house was completed. Sonia sat in her lounge. She felt happy. The house would be let, and she could relax at last. She picked up her sewing bag. She needed to crochet. She would start a new jumper. Crochet made her happy. She could not find the crochet hook she needed. The ones in her sewing bag were either too big or too small. Where was her size four hook? Then she remembered that she had taken the hook to her friend's house, as her friend needed some crochet around the edge of a blanket she was making. Sonia had offered to do it, for the price of a cup of tea, some cake and a pleasant afternoon of chat and laughter. She wondered, could the hook be in one of her coat pockets?

She went to the hall cupboard to look. Several coats were hung on top of each other. She worked her way through them. As she put her hand into the pocket of her red duffle coat, she became aware. She opened her eyes and raised her eyebrows. She had not found her crochet hook but … a disturbing realisation suddenly hit her. She then screwed up her eyes, scrunched up her forehead and began to consider what she should do next. She was worried. Her fingers were feeling the smoothness of an envelope. It was the envelope of the letter Mark had left for her in his room. She had forgotten all about it. She pulled it out of her coat pocket and just stared at it.

Immediately after Mark's death she had decided not to give the letter to the police, nor to open it herself. Consequently she had done nothing with it. She had just forgotten about it. Now she was feeling differently. Now she wanted to know if it held anything relevant to Mark's suicide. She felt she could deal with it now. Knowledge is a valuable commodity. She no longer felt afraid of any repercussions. Anyway, if she didn't like what it contained, she could just lose it again. Her search for the crochet hook was aborted and Sonia carefully began to open the envelope. She wondered what she would find. She felt a strange excitement as she looked at the white paper and read the words …

Dear Sonia,

Please forgive me for laying so much at your door. You are the only person I know who would understand what I have been feeling. You are the only person I have shared my history with. You know about my Jo.

By now you will know about my suicide. Because of my work, I anticipated that my colleagues would have considered the possibility of it being a staged suicide. So many things seem to be pointing towards Russia at the moment.

Also, I feared that they may have suspected Tom. This is why I am writing to you. Tom was not involved. I had been suspicious of him myself. I am suspicious of most things. I had discovered that Tom was not what he seemed to be. I found out some things about him. I still have contacts in the British Government and American Intelligence Agencies. Tom is OK and he had nothing to do with my demise. He works for the Slovakian police. He had come from Slovakia regarding a death that had happened in some caves. He thought I might have had something to do with the death. Anyway, we did have a confrontation, during which Tom came clean. I knew I had nothing to do with any deaths in Slovakia or anywhere else for that matter. It was then that he told me that the person who had died was from the Government Intelligence Agency. It was my Jo.

Needless to say, I was devastated. I could not breathe. I could not believe that the love of my life no longer shared this world with me. I had some months ago received a letter from Jo. After all this time he had contacted me to tell me he had fallen in love with a woman who worked at his gym, he called her his Green Enchantress. We were communicating regularly. He was trusting me and sharing things about his life. I was over the moon. To be told he was dead was too much to bear. I knew such news would bring on my dangling depression. I knew I could not let this decline become slow decay. I needed to exit. If my love could not share this world with me, then I would share his world with him.

So, please Sonia. If there is any suspicion around Tom please show this letter to the police.

Be happy in the knowledge that I have done everything in my power to be with Jo. I will be dancing with him in Never Never Land. I will be with him for all eternity. This Lost Boy will be flying again with his Peter Pan.

Thank you for your understanding.

Mark.

PS (1) Jo told me that the woman, Jo's Green Enchantress, had cast an entangled emerald enchantment over him. It's so romantic isn't it!

(2) Having found me and realised that I had nothing to do with Jo's death, Tom, whose real name is Metod, intended to look for her. I wonder if she knows anything about his death? This might be a pregnant area for enquiry? Apparently, she is tall, beautiful, and bright, and she likes to wear green glasses! So, perhaps, on second thoughts, it is best if you let the police see this letter. They will then decide what to do.

Sonia slowly walked into the lounge, placed the letter on her coffee table and moved towards her phone. It was time to phone her kind coroner again. Appropriately, Justin Bieber's 'Ghost' was playing on the radio. She realised that Mark had experienced what Justin was singing about in the song. His suicide had been because he missed Jo 'more than life'. She felt dismayed as she considered that now Jo and Mark were both ensconced in the world of ghosts. A sad ending to a sorry tale.

She turned the radio off and picked up the phone. Her friendly coroner listened to her account, then told her not to worry he would sort it all out. She felt he was always 'sorting things out' for her, and she suspected for everyone else as well.

Later that day, the scarecrows were knocking on her front door yet again. This time she was ready for them. This time she was stronger. Like before she showed them into her lounge. When they were seated, she gave them Mark's letter. She was prepared to be in trouble. She had withheld evidence yet again. She knew she may well face prosecution. Despite all of this she felt that she had to honour Mark's wishes. After all, she had already lost his ashes. Perhaps this was one way in which she could compensate for her apparent lack of vigilance. A way to make amends for spoiling his last earthly journey by carelessly leaving him sitting alone on her passenger seat without any protection.

Sonia decided to tell the scarecrows how she had put the letter in her pocket and then had just forgotten about it. That would do. That indeed was nearly the truth. To her amazement they seemed to accept this explanation. Maybe they were being kind, or maybe they just realised how old, and forgetful she had become. Whatever the reason, Sonia was relieved that they seemed to not be interested in taking any further steps to prosecute her for withholding evidence. They only seemed interested in tracing Tom or the woman who had been mentioned in the letter. The so-called Green Enchantress. Sonia hoped that there had been no enchantments taking place. She was usually quite fearful of supernatural occurrences. However, thankfully the scarecrows held no such fears. They were intent on their work. They needed to find an earthly Tom and a Green Enchantress from Slovakia. The letter had given them a starting point. The woman worked at the gym where Jo was a member. The scarecrows left.

The next day, the Metropolitan Police started looking for Tom. Tom, aka Metod was soon found. He seemed to have disappeared following Mark's suicide, but he was easily tracked to a London hotel. After his confrontation with Mark, Metod had realised that Mark had not been involved with Jo's death. His thoughts were redirected to the woman sharing the flat and possibly owning the green glasses. He would need to track her down.

Metod reflected on what he had accomplished already and congratulated himself on finding Mark … He looked at notebook where he logged his progress.

'On initially arriving in England I visited my colleagues at the Metropolitan Police in London. After explaining the situation regarding the body in the lake they did not seem interested. I decided to carry out my own enquiries. My contacts at the Government Intelligence Agency were more helpful. They soon provided me with Mark's address in Cheltenham. They also said that it was a house of multiple occupancy and that a room was currently being advertised. I quickly followed their lead and visited the address they had given. Within the first week of arriving in England I had moved into the house and begun observing Mark. I set myself up as a window cleaner. Things seemed to be going smoothly. My enquiries regarding Mark continued. I tried to befriend him. It seemed he had not been out of the country for some time. I could not find any link between Mark and the cave incident. Eventually he became irritated by my questions and we had an argument. I came clean and told him who I was and about the body which had been discovered in the lake. I knew Mark could not have been involved in the lake incident, nor would he be able to give me any further information. I would no longer spend any time considering Mark's involvement. I now needed to concentrate on the woman sharing the flat in Poprad.'

Metod was pleased with his work so far. However, finding the woman sharing the flat with Jo was proving to be more problematic. He needed to find her. She was the missing link.

Knowing there was no legitimate reason to remain in England, Metod decided to return to Slovakia. Metod enjoyed being in England, but he knew he must return home. However, a couple of days sightseeing would not hurt anyone. Two days later, Tom the window cleaner became Metod the detective again. He was on an early flight back to Bratislava. He needed to find the woman.

Fortunately, now that the police had Mark's letter, things started to move. The next week saw the Metropolitan Police and the Slovakian Police working together. Information was being shared and resources allocated. Metod was delighted. When Metod's colleagues at the Government Intelligence Agency realised that it was Jo's body which had been found in the lake they explained that the make-up was most probably Jo's and that he had lived at the flat alone. Things were progressing.

Despite all the information given to him regarding Jo's delight in wearing make-up, Metod was still not convinced. He found it difficult to comprehend that any man would use such a vast range of make-up and perfumes. He was still inclined to search for the woman living at the flat with Jo.

The investigation moved on as lines of enquiry were developed. Both the English and the Slovakian police found the fact that green glasses were discovered by the body to be a possible lead. They also now knew that Jo had been in love with a woman from the gym he was attending. Now, they were all trying to discover who she was, this woman with green glasses. This woman Jo called his Green Enchantress. A Green Enchantress who had cast an entangled emerald enchantment over him. She needed to be found.

Following his return to his homeland, Metod did not ask the local police to check out the gyms in Poprad. He felt he knew that Jo would have joined AquaCity. He had previously seen pairs of swimming trunks on the chair in Jo's flat and a flyer advertising AquaCity classes. It had to be AquaCity. Metod wanted to visit AquaCity personally. He wanted to be the man to discover the Green Enchantress.

On a bright Tuesday morning, a car carrying Metod and another detective from Bratislava pulled up outside the large swimming complex. They were soon sitting in the small office, to the rear of the reception hall, questioning the manager about his staff. It was eventually established that a woman who wore green glasses had worked at the City, but that she had left. The manager gave the detectives all the information he had regarding Martina. One key piece of information made our two detectives look knowingly at each other. Martina had terminated her employment shortly before the date that the body had been discovered in the lake. According to the forensic team, the time frame of her departure corresponded to the time frame for the window of death of the body in the lake. The investigations were moving forward well. Metod was optimistic as he stood up to leave. The manager then said,

'I was annoyed that she left so abruptly. She was a fairly good worker and if anything went wrong with the equipment she would try to fix it. I was aware of something strange about her though. I could not put my finger on it. She had no friends here and she would suddenly seem to be angry for no apparent reason. At times I felt uncomfortable when she was talking to me. She would fix the equipment, yet I always felt she needed fixing herself. Hey, this track reminds me of her!'

The manager moved to the music system and selected the chosen track. 'The Fixer' by Brent Morgan resonated from all the speakers around the complex. The detectives listened, smiled and then left the room followed by the manager. They thanked him for his help and returned to their car in order to drive to the address they had been given. Twenty minutes later they entered the village where Martina's parents lived.

It was a pleasant village surrounded by green fields and numerous trees. There were about two hundred houses, each with large gardens. Most of the gardens were full of all sorts of vegetables and herbs. The sound of crowing cockerels came from different directions at differing times throughout the day.

The house belonging to Martina's parents was in a road which led down to the railway line. There was no official stop for the trains, but the locals knew that if you just waited by the railway sign and raised your hand as the train approached, the driver would stop and let you board. Trains, whilst being efficient ways to travel from one part of the country to another, were still quite unregulated. They had both a driver and a conductor. In between the official stations, there were many small villages needing servicing. When passing these small villages the driver and the conductor would be in control of when and where the train would stop and who would be allowed to board. It was an efficient way of ensuring most people using the trains were relatively happy.

The house was large. A glass porch protected the front door whilst the side garden was a maze of hand-built pens and cages housing rabbits, chickens and pigs. Two friendly dogs ran to meet the detectives as they approached the porch and rang the bell. Hands were licked, coats ruffled and sounds of the Slovakian for 'what a good dog' were heard. The detectives were welcomed.

Following the decision of his two discerning dogs to allow these unknown men onto the property, Martina's father opened the front door. After receiving introductions and evidence of their position as detectives, he invited them into the house. The large hallway was lined with dark wooden panels and equally dark furniture. The windows were hung with handmade ecru cotton lace curtains. An ornate table sat in the middle of the hall, upon which stood a vase of wildflowers. The wooden tabletop had been decorated with a hot polka to give the impression of leaves and flowers being drawn all over the surface. They were ushered through the hall and into the lounge where Martina's mother was seated on the sofa, knitting.

They all sat down as Martina's parents looked at each other, wondering why detectives would need to visit their home. At the back of their minds they suspected it would have to be something to do with their daughter. Not the daughter who was currently tending the vegetable plot at the rear of the house, but the wayward daughter who had left for pastures new.

An hour of interrogation and much anxiety on the part of the two unsuspecting parents resulted in them sharing the knowledge that their daughter had worn green glasses, she had worked at the AquaCity and she had left home. However, though they did not know where she had gone, she had taken her passport. They thought she might have gone to England. Her sister had been at a party chatting to the young man who worked in the travel shop. He had told her that Martina had bought a ticket to London, England. However, they were not absolutely sure as they had heard nothing from her since she left.

Our detectives left the house with smiles on their faces. They tickled the dogs as they were escorted by their canine companions to the gate. They returned to their car and smiled at each other as they both realised they were now on the track of the owner of the green glasses. Metod felt particularly happy. It seemed this woman, called Martina, had left for London. He would need to return to England.

England would hold the answers he required surrounding the body in the Emerald Lake. He needed to know more about the entangled emerald enchantments that surrounded the death of Jo. He was sure that he would find Jo's Green Enchantress in England. Metod was resigned. He would leave for England immediately and track down the owner of the green glasses. He was determined to find this Martina …

CHAPTER THIRTEEN

METOD RETURNS TO ENGLAND

'My past is everything I failed to be.'
Fernando Pessoa, *The Book of Disquiet*

At last things were settling down for the Slovakian police. Metod's superiors seemed pleased with the work he had undertaken. He had traced the owner of the green glasses and he had discovered that she had most probably left the country and gone to England. The case could be closed. It would look good on the monthly statistics to show a closed case. Also the enquiries were becoming very expensive and using too much of the ever dwindling police budget. Jo's death could be recorded as an accident. It was a good result. Metod's superiors were content.

However, Metod was far from content. He still had many unanswered questions. He could not wipe away his concerns of yesterday in order to placate his superiors and close the file on Jo's demise. He still wondered how Jo had entered the caves and why Martina's green glasses had been found next to the body. If both Jo and Martina had been together in the caves and it had simply been an accident, surely Martina would have alerted the guides and tried to get Jo out of the Emerald Lake's waters. Also, why had she left the country so quickly after the so called 'accident' if she had nothing to fear? Things were not adding up.

Metod was an insightful detective. He would consider different approaches to his work. He would always try to think 'outside the box'. He would question and ponder. He would imagine and challenge. However, despite all his mental considerations, he had one attribute that always stood him in good stead. He had hackles. Ever since he was a child he would feel the hackles at the back of his neck shivering if things were amiss. He was so sure of his intuitive response to people and situations that he never questioned his abilities. If his hackles rose then he was one hundred percent sure that something was wrong.

As he offered his report to his boss he knew his hackles were pushing him to take it further. He did not want to accept that the case was closed. He knew he had to continue and at least find Martina. He hoped that she might be able to explain what had occurred in the caves and why her green glasses had been found by the side of Jo's body.

The file sat on the table between Metod and his boss. Metod failed to hear his boss congratulate him on a job well done. All he could consider was how he was going to keep the case open. Suddenly, inspiration invaded his thoughts as he found himself saying,

'Yes, we have achieved much already. I am glad that we were able to trace the owner of the glasses. When I was in England and talking to my colleagues at the Government Intelligence Agency they thought we would never trace the owner. They seemed to be very dismissive of the ability of our police force. Finding that Jo worked for them and had been doing covert surveillance for so long did come as a shock to me. We had no idea that he was living in Poprad, nor that he was liaising with those in Ukraine. I think the English thought that Martina was involved in some way.

They seemed to want to find her too. They were not happy that we had not been able to find her.'

That did the job. His superior had been challenged. The Slovakian police had been insulted by some English boffins who spent all their time listening to private conversations. He had heard that most of the people working at the Government Intelligence Agency were rather unusual to say the least; and for them to question and to be dismissive regarding the abilities of his police force was unacceptable.

The next moment Metod was being instructed to leave Slovakia and head for England. Martina must be found. She must be found by the Slovakian police. She must be questioned regarding the death of Jo. The Slovakian police would tie up all the ends surrounding the mystery. After all they had already done all the ground work. The only thing which remained was a simple interview with this woman who owned the green glasses. Then the case could be closed. It was not for the English to interview her. Metod was to find her and finish his report following her interview.

Both Metod and his boss looked at each other and smiled. They would ensure that the reputation of the Slovakian police remained intact.

The file was handed back to him and Metod left the office. He had achieved what he wanted. He would return to England and find this woman called Martina. Only after discovering her would he feel able to close the case. He needed his questions answered and she was the one person who knew the answers.

The only clue that Metod had found was that Martina was thought to have bought a ticket to London. He was well aware of the size of that capital city. Looking for her would be problematic. He needed something to go on. He wondered if her family would be able to offer any further help.

That afternoon he returned to the house belonging to Martina's parents. The dogs ran to meet him as he opened the gate. Licks, stokes and sweet nothings passed between them. He rang the door bell. Martina's sister opened the door. She smiled sweetly as she explained that her parents were out visiting friends, but they were expected back within the hour.

'May I come in and wait for them? I am trying to trace your sister. She seems to have disappeared. We need to check that she is OK.'

Metod moved forward as he spoke, entering the dark wood panelled hallway and closing the front door behind him. He gave no opportunity for her to refuse his request.

'Well I suppose you can wait in the lounge. They should not be too long,' she purred.

Martina's sister was compliant. She led him into the lounge. Metod looked at her. She was delicate and pale. Her hair which was tied at the back of her head in a black scrunchie was ash blonde. It reached her waist. Her eyes were a strange pale violet colour and her nails were painted a pearly white. She wore faded jeans and a simple white tee shirt. The slippers on her feet were bright pink and were made of fluffy nylon fur which had seen better days.

'Would you like a cup of tea? I have just made some fresh mint tea,' she asked, knowing the importance of being polite to any visitors who graced her parent's front door.

Metod accepted and a few minutes later he was sitting on a comfortable sofa and relaxing in the sunlight which flowed into the room.

It was a large room. One wall was covered by glass fronted cabinets full of ornate crystal from the Czech Republic. This Bohemia Crystal was expensive to buy. Martina's parents had inherited some from their parents, when Czechoslovakia existed. Since 1 January 1993, following the dissolution of Czechoslovakia into the Czech Republic and Slovakia, they would travel across the border and try to purchase odd pieces for their collection. Plates of all sizes, glasses and ornaments filled the shelves. It was an impressive collection.

Metod liked the old-fashioned formality of the room. It reminded him of his grandparents' home. Even the smell of wax polish transported him to days spent playing on the wooden floor of their dining room when he was an infant. The house belonging to Martina's parents made him feel comfortable. He closed his eyes and awaited the arrival of the mint tea.

Soon Martina's sister was entering the room again carrying a formica tray with two large cups of tea and some delicate home-made coconut biscuits. The pottery of the cups, saucers and tea plates was matching. It was white bone china covered with pink rosebuds and green leaves. Again, he was returned to his grandparents' house. They had had identical china wear. He pondered. Perhaps this was a relic of the communist days when most people had limited choice regarding their purchases. There was never the range of options which was evident nowadays. He remembered that his grandparents had wanted to remain within the safe confines of communism. They had always been assured of jobs. They had been given housing. They wanted for nothing. Yet at one time their fridge had broken down. They had to wait for nearly a year for a replacement to arrive. So, there were obviously some limitations to their idealised view of life under a communist regime.

His mind returned to his work. He began drinking his tea. Martina's sister, Anna, smiled sweetly as he praised who ever had made the delicious coconut biscuits.

'Oh, I made them. I love cooking. My parents say that I'm a super cook. I can make most things taste wonderful. I am glad you like them. Martina could not cook. Despite being older than me she really did not do much about the house. I am well prepared. My parents say I am a credit to them. I am to be married shortly and I feel confident that I will be able to run my own house well. I am looking forward to it.'

Metod returned Anna's smile, thinking to himself that she was more talkative than he had originally realised. He also sensed a slight sibling rivalry towards Martina. Maybe Anna would have some information about her sister? He began,

'I suppose you are very worried about your sister. It is strange that she seems to have disappeared and no one knows where she is?'

'You are mistaken. She is not my real sister. We have no blood ties. We look nothing like each other, and she is much older than me. My parents adopted her when she was four. They did not think they were able to have children of their own. They had been trying for so long. Anyway, some years later my mum got pregnant with me. It was too late to return her. Apparently she had been returned many times before she was given to my parents. She seemed to be always getting into trouble as an infant. Now she is still getting into trouble as an adult.'

Anna's reply reinforced Metod's initial assumption. She did not like Martina. He asked what she meant by getting into trouble as an adult.

'Far be it for me to gossip, but my dear parents have had a dreadful time with Martina. She was going to be a dancer. They paid a fortune for dance lessons for her. But then she had an accident and was unable to dance. She caused the accident. It was all her fault. Now she is banned from driving. She has never really contributed much to the family, and she has had so many failed relationships that I don't think she knows how to behave or even keep a man. My dad says she is wanton and reckless. He says she has unnatural appetites. She dabbles in things that are strange. Our Catholic priest once did an exorcism on her, but I don't think it worked. Do you know, she never brings any of her boyfriends home. She just seems to make a mess of all her relationships. The only thing she does well is to keep her room tidy. Everything is in its place and it's all so clean. She cleans it herself and won't let us go in. Would you like to see it? It really is quite unbelievable how tidy it is.'

Not wanting to offend Martina's non-sister, Metod nodded his head. She left the room and he followed. Upstairs there appeared to be four large bedrooms. Anna opened the first door on the right. The room looked like something from a well-designed hospital. Not a thing was out of place. There were no books or ornaments, only a very large clock on the wall opposite the bed and a pack of Tarot cards on the bedside table. Everything was white or pale green. It was a clinical experience, void of dirt, design or decoration. Metod was lost for words. There was nothing to comment upon. The room had nothing to recommend it to the onlooker. It was a sterile space. He groped for something to say which did not sound negative. Finally he looked again at the clock mounted on the wall.

'What a large clock,' Metod observed.

'Time was always very important to Martina. She had to have her day organised into different time periods. She was more aware of time than the trains leaving the stations. Everything was done to time. When she was working at the school she would wake up extra early every day and clean her room from top to bottom before she left for work. I liked it when she worked at the school. She would be away from the house for most of the day. My parents liked it too. We were all upset when she was forced to leave. Something dreadful happened at the school. I expect you read about it in the papers?'

Anna continued. Metod could not believe his luck. This non-sister was so keen to share not only her own thoughts, but the thoughts of her parents too. She was giving him a rich, if somewhat skewed picture of Martina's life. It was as if Anna was a clockwork toy which had been wound up and released, unable to stop until the tightly wound spring had become completely undone. She seemed delighted to be able to run her sister, sorry non-sister, down.

'Thank you for showing me.'

He left the room. It held no clues to Martina's whereabouts, but it did tell him something about her personality and life style. They both returned to the lounge. Metod continued his questioning.

'I suppose Martina will be returning for your wedding soon.'

'I very much doubt it. She has not been in touch since she left. She just went and she took my mum's jewellery with her. She also took all the money from their account. She really is not welcome here anymore. My parents say we are better off as a family without her. I just wish ...'

Anna's wishing was brought to an abrupt end as her mother entered the room.

'Oh, I wondered who was talking. I could hear voices when I put my key in the front door. I was not expecting visitors.'

Metod stood up and apologised for the intrusion.

'I had some more questions for you regarding Martina's disappearance. Your daughter has been very hospitable and welcoming. We have shared some fresh mint tea and coconut biscuits. She is an excellent hostess.'

Anna's mum smiled adoringly at her daughter as her husband joined the group. Metod again explained that he had some questions that needed answering and he hoped they would be able to help him.

Anna exited to the kitchen to make more tea, as the others sat down. General chatter began, though both parents looked concerned. Metod was aware that they seemed to be uncomfortable with his presence. He asked them again if they had any idea where Martina could be staying, perhaps staying in London. Did they have any relatives there? Did Martina know any British people who she could be visiting?

Nothing seemed to be forthcoming from either parent. As Anna brought their teas into the room, Metod stood up and thanking them for their time he began walking towards the door. Anna put her tray down and escorted him to the front door.

'Thank you for your kind hospitality and the delicious coconut biscuits. Here is my number if Martina does contact you.'

He handed her his card. After he had left the building, once again the two dogs escorted him along the path to the front gate.

Anna waved graciously from the still open front door.

She shouted after him.

'Jacob at the travel shop may know something. He got her the ticket to London. I think she had a fling with him too.'

Anna then closed the door and returned to her responsibilities of delighting her adoring parents.

Metod felt sorry for Martina. He was glad that he did not have a perfect sister like Anna. He got in his car and set off for the travel agents. Maybe Jacob would indeed know something useful.

The travel shop was small but very clean and tidy, as was Jacob. Metod looked at the young man sitting behind his desk. He was immaculate. His hair was short with a quiff at the front. He was dressed in a crisp blue gingham shirt and his trousers were a white twill with turn-ups. He was obviously into fashion.

'Can I help you?' were the first words Metod heard.

The young man was polite and eager to help as Metod explained the reason for his visit. It was soon confirmed that he had purchased the ticket for Martina. Then the enquires took a more personal turn, as Metod asked.

'I believe you were romantically involved with Martina?'

The reply was immediate, though he sounded irritated by the question.

'I would not say romantically involved. I doubt that she could be romantically involved with anyone. I have met toxic women like her before; they lure you with sex and then treat you badly. I was prepared. She could not fool me. But I must admit she did seem more toxic than most. We had a fling. But it was just physical. In fact, it was only physical. She seemed to have no capacity for anything else. I tried talking to her. She seemed to want to keep everything a secret. I think there was something really wrong with her. If I disagreed with what she wanted she would get so angry and scream at me. She even hit me. It was all very strange. I have never been with a girl that bad before. She was on some sort of medication. But I also think that she was using something, not sure what. I have never been involved in drugs or anything like that. Anyway, we only went out for about four weeks. In fact, we didn't 'go out'. She would come here as the shop was closing and we would go to the shower room at the back. She told me that she was as powerful at the lightning bolt tattoo on her wrist. She was really odd. We never went anywhere. I enjoyed being with her for the physical contact but there was nothing else. But that was all it was, nothing more. She did not tell me where she was going in London. So really I cannot help you. But if you do find her be sure not to upset her as she can be really nasty at times.'

Metod listened to the response brought about by his simple question. It seemed that the Martina he was seeking was quite a handful. A handful for both her family and her boyfriends. Whilst finding out much about the woman who had lost her green glasses, Metod felt he was still a long way off from finding her. He felt he was failing. There had been no clues as to her whereabouts. He needed to consider another option.

London would be the answer. He would reconnect with the Metropolitan Police. They would help him find her. He left the travel shop and returned home to pack.

CHAPTER FOURTEEN

FEAR AND FRUSTRATION IN LONDON

'To wipe everything from the slate from one day to the next, to be new with each new morning, in a perpetually restored virginity of emotion – this and only this is worth being or having.'

Fernando Pessoa, *The Book of Disquiet*

Metod tried to feel positive as he greeted his new day. He pushed his feelings of failure to the back of his mind and focused on how he would navigate his time in London. His flight to Heathrow was uneventful. Metod was soon removing his clothes from his compact suitcase. He had taken a small room at one of the airport's chain hotels. He hung the few clothes he had brought with him on the rail in the corner which had been designed to hold hangers for odd garments. There was no room for a wardrobe in this efficient bedroom. The hotel had been a good choice. It was clean, cheap and not too far from the more expensive hotels situated in central London. He could access most of London easily. There were many buses and tubes from Heathrow into the centre of the capital. He showered and returned to the Marks and Spencer food outlet in the terminal building, buying some sandwiches, an iced coffee and a ready-made salad. He then sat to drink a coffee before heading into central London.

He soon found police headquarters. All the police who had helped in the initial investigations regarding Mark were not available. They had either been moved to other areas or were just absent or on holiday. There seemed to be some resistance to continuing with any investigations regarding Mark and his death. After being passed from one detective to another, Metod realised that the Metropolitan Police did not want to become involved in searching for Martina. He felt that he would get no support from his London colleagues. He would need to find her himself.

Knowing that she had worked at AquaCity, Metod deduced that she might be looking for work in a similar field. Anna had said that she had emptied her parent's accounts. Anna had also told him that she had taken all her mum's jewellery. She did have money and jewellery to sell, but knowing the cost of things in London he knew eventually she would be forced to look for work.

He began contacting gyms in the capital. He could not believe how many gyms there were. It seemed that London was full of overweight, unconditioned people seeking to redress their overeating and sedentary work styles by spending evenings working out. He did not have much to go on. Martina had not touched her own bank account since leaving Slovakia, nor had she used her phone. He suspected she would have purchased another mobile on her arrival in England. He continued his phone search, ringing different gyms, asking if any new female trainers had been taken on within the last few weeks. Four days of negative responses left him feeling flat. He began to think that he may never find her.

Five days into his London sojourn he stuck lucky. A small gym near St Pancras station had taken on a new trainer just four weeks earlier. The description seemed to fit that of Martina. Metod felt a frisson of excitement as he made arrangements to visit the gym later in the day, telling the manager not to mention anything to the woman in question. Plodding police methods are always the best, ran through his mind as he took the local underground to St Pancras station.

The gym was a small unit behind a fast-food outlet, just off the main road. It was equipped with all the latest equipment and had two shower rooms, plus toilets at the rear. It was exceptionally clean and well designed for such a small venue. One area had been sectioned off. This was deemed the 'workout and dance' space. On seeing Metod's official identification the manager immediately became co-operative. He did not want any trouble. His was a respectable gym. The woman in question, who had given her name as Tina, seemed a decent person. He had interview her himself.

'Where was her last job,' Metod asked.

'I can't remember but there were very good references,' the manager lied.

He had seen no references. Had been so short staffed he would have employed a known serial killer to cover the classes. He had not even asked her for references. She was given the job with no references and very little to prove that she could actually teach classes. Lucky for the manager, Martina, or Tina as she was now known, was a good teacher and she enjoyed taking the classes. It had been a successful transaction.

'How do you pay her,' Metod asked, feeling that he had found his mark at last.

'She said she had only arrived in the country recently, so she had no bank account. I paid her weekly by cash. She said that would be OK until she had got a place to live and established herself. I will sort it all out as soon as she lets me have a reference and a bank account. I don't know where she is staying. I think she is looking for accommodation.'

The two men looked knowingly at each other. Both being suspicious, both knowing that paying someone cash was not a good idea. It could be viewed as a black market transaction. However, Metod did not want to challenge the manager. He needed his co-operation.

Metod needed to meet this woman who had recently started working at the gym. He felt sure it must be the Martina he was looking for. After asking when she was next due at work he was told it would be Friday. Two days away. The manager did not know where she lived, or what her phone number was. It was all very suspicious. Still Metod could do nothing until he had been able to talk to her and ask her about Jo and the Slovakian caves. Patience, the word rang around Metod's head. He would have to be patient.

Most police officers would have continued searching, just in case Tina was not the Martina they were seeking. Most police officers would have continued ringing around the remaining gyms and asking if they had taken on any new staff. Metod was different. Metod felt that his intuition told him that he had found her. He trusted his feelings. He did not need to look further. He just had to wait until Friday when he would be able to confront her at the gym. He thanked the manager for his help, adding that nothing was to be said to the woman in question. He then returned to his room, where a large bottle of duty-free whisky sat next to the tea and coffee making facilities. He would have a shower, watch TV, and gradually drink himself into a pleasant stupor, watch a movie and then have a night full of happy dreams. His plans were made.

The next morning our clever detective awoke late with a throbbing head. What had seemed desirable last night was now considered a stupid activity. The bottle lay on the floor.

Had he drunk a whole bottle, or had it just spilled out and dried in the night? His head did not belong to him. He regretted his actions. The day was spent drinking coffee and wishing he had been more sensible. He had lost a whole day. A whole day when he could have been sightseeing in one of his favourite cities. Twenty-four hours later he was up with the lark and heading for the river. He would take a ride on one of the river boats to Greenwich. He loved the river and all its murky history. He passed Traitors Gate and wondered at the thoughts of those historical figures who had been forced through its portals. He looked in awe at Tower Bridge. Nowhere in the world was there such a beautiful and decorative bridge. London was magical for Metod. The bustle and the buildings delighted his desire to be in the midst of everything. He loved Bratislava; the castle, the museum, the Opera House and even the train station. But it did not have the noise and bustle of London.

The people in London seemed to come from all parts of the world. He would hear many different languages spoken on the streets, and in the shops and restaurants. Most people in London either spoke a different language or had a strange accent. He loved the cosmopolitan nature of this vibrant city. Although he was keen to find and interview Martina he was grateful to be able to have time to just enjoy the excitement that London offered.

He spent the afternoon in the National Gallery and then moved on to explore the Portrait Gallery. He wondered where the extra-long escalators, which seemed to rise into heaven from the Portrait Gallery, led. His inquisitive nature forced him to join the first metallic step on the over-extended escalators. Soon he found himself at the top, looking into a space full of tables and chairs. It was a restaurant. Before he realised what was happening a super-efficient waiter had led him to a table by the window.

'This is one of our best views. You can see so much from here. Would you like just tea and cake or our full afternoon tea menu, which includes sandwiches as well?'

Metod seemed mesmerised by the view. The only words he could muster were, 'Yes please.'

The waiter left, obviously happy with the affirmation from his recently captured diner.

Soon Metod was sitting in front of a magnificent, tiered display of small triangular shaped sandwiches, scones, jam, butter and cream, plus an assortment of delicate 'fancies'. He had not come across fancies before. On asking the waiter what the word meant, he was told it referred to an assortment of iced and cream small cakes of different shapes and flavours.

'They are all delicious,' the eager waiter assured him.

A silver tea pot, jug of hot water and a small jug of milk surrounded the bone china tea cup and saucer, which completed the tableau.

Metod was content. He enjoyed acting like an English gentleman and he relished the English elegant way of life. 'Afternoon tea should be compulsory,' he thought to himself. 'The world would be a much happier place, if everyone stopped everything they were doing at four o'clock and just sat down to take afternoon tea and cake.'

Metod really enjoyed his time spent in London. He was confident he would find Martina on Friday and she would be able to explain how her green glasses had come to be found next to Jo's body in the cave. He would tie up all the ends of the case, return to Slovakia and his mind would be at rest. His superiors would be delighted with his work and the

Metropolitan Police, plus all the boffins at the Government Intelligence Agency, would have no reason to even consider that the Slovakian police were anything other than super-efficient. Life was going well.

He had been correct. It was Martina who had taken the job at the gym. What he did not know was that already she had become involved with two people. First she had targeted one of the other workers; a young and handsome trainer who immediately fell under her spell. She knew how to attract men. She could be enchanting. It was all too easy for her. She had done it so many times before. She would look into their eyes and flatter them. She would giggle at their jokes. She would touch them gently without appearing too forward. Soon she was moving towards her newly found mark and cuddling into his strong body. He was eager to know her. Eager to feel more of her tantalising strokes on his arms as he lifted his body and did twenty press-ups. He was fit and well able to prove to her how adept he was at satisfying an equally fit woman. She had soon beguiled him. After his work-out Martina followed him into the showers and their relationship was assured. They were both happy as they listened to Ed Sheeran singing 'Bad Habits' on the sound system. They both laughed. She knew he could fulfil her immediate needs. She could be assured of his attention whilst working at the gym. Sadly he did not work at the gym every day. Martina's appetite necessitated daily atten-tion. She would need somebody else to gratify her needs.

Martina's mind had dismissed the time she had spent with Jo. He was forgotten. She had also forgotten how she felt when she was with him. It seemed that she would just move on from one conquest to another. She was back to relying on superficial sexual encounters for gratification. She could not afford the luxury of memory. It was as if her mind just moved onto future targets, to fulfilling her immediate needs, whilst forgetting all previous liaisons.

She needed another partner to play with her in the showers. She needed someone to fill in the days when she was alone. She had come across her second mark quite by accident. During one of her Zumba classes a woman at the back had twisted her foot. She had to sit out for the remainder of the class. When the session had finished Martina went to check to see if she was alright. There appeared to be no bones broken, but some spraining. Martina got a wet cold tea towel and put it on the woman's ankle. As she leant over, the woman placed her hand on Martina's head and gently stroked her hair. Both women paused. It was a strange interaction. Martina remembered a childhood experience when a woman, presumably her mother had stroked her hair and kissed her gently on the top of her head. Martina looked at the woman, who was called Pat. They smiled and then kissed. Martina had been with many women before, but this woman seemed different. She was much older than Martina and although Martina liked to be in total control of her sexual encounters, she seemed to feel comfortable with letting this woman take the lead. The woman put her arms around Martina and began kissing and caressing her. Fortunately, everyone else had left the dance area. They were alone. The woman's foot appeared to be recovered as she and Martina moved towards the showers. They showered together and enjoyed the closeness.

Martina felt good. She knew she now had two people who could supply what she needed.

Each time she took a class at the gym she would find one of her two playmates ready to share a shower with her.

She was delighted that life seemed to be working out for her. Though she neither cared nor wondered about her play-mates, the woman did offer her some interesting news. The woman explained that she was a psychopharmacologist.

'What's that?' was Martina's quick reply. 'Are you a psycho?'

The woman laughed, telling Martina that she was basically a psychiatrist who would consider what various medications could do to the body and how medications could affect each other. She was a sort of super psychiatrist with knobs on but definitely not psychotic. She then laughed as she added,

'Actually we can all be psychos at times, even you!'

Martina was not sure what she meant. Her lack of laughter and the confused expression on her face caused Pat to add,

'Tina, I understand what you are dealing with. On a more serious note, I can help you with medication. I can make life easier for you. We will be good for each other.'

She told Martina, or Tina, that she fully understood about her condition. That she had treated many individuals with similar conditions. Martina was at first fearful. What was this psychiatrist talking about? What conditions? Not another 'professional' like the ones her parents had insisted that she visit? She did not want nor need another 'professional' in her life. However, she felt she wanted this woman. She wanted to continue seeing this woman. Her physical needs overtook her indignation. She would continue seeing this psychiatrist on her own terms. Martina decided that she would dismiss what the psychiatrist had said about her 'condition'. In future, she would only make idle conversation with her. They would share showers together and nothing more. Martina would get all she needed in the shower and that would be an end to it. No discussions or disclosures.

Psychiatry is not a precise science. The psychiatry of personality disorders can sometimes be viewed as not being a science at all. Our psychiatrist had worked for many years trying to unravel the complications of her clients. She had learnt much through her wide ranging experience. She found her clients fascinating. Her focus on personality disorders allowed her to meet and explore many intriguing individuals. She had been drawn to Martina from the first time she observed her. However, she was alert enough to realise that Martina would not thank her for wanting to 'help'. She knew that most neurotypicals would usually feel obliged to help neurodivergents. Fortunately, current clinical considerations included the view that perhaps those with some types of personality disorder should not be viewed as needing treatment, but rather as just another way of being. She wondered if this new way of viewing personality disorders was just a reaction to both psychiatrists and psychologists knowing that they could only offer limited treatment for some conditions. She knew that many professionals were refusing to work with individuals who had been diagnosed with Borderline Personality Disorder. One school of thought suggested that perhaps those with certain 'disorders' should just be avoided as nothing could be done for them. She, on the other hand, always felt willing to try to help young and usually beautiful women with their challenges.

In her practice she tried to focus on the positive attributes of her clients. Recently there had been much negative press and stigma around those with so called personality disorders. Much of the literature offered generalisations suggesting that clients could be labelled as being manipulative and untrustworthy. Many could have relationship problems due to their inability to regulate their emotions. For others their impulsivity and sexual disinhibition was often viewed as problematic. The fields of both psychiatry and psychology were becoming more complex with each decade.

However our enlighten psychopharmacologist always attempted to see her clients in a positive light. She observed Martina. She became aware of her enthusiasm and passion for her work. Martina always attempted to ensure that all her classes were fun experiences. She would give of her all, offering support and encouragement to those around her. The so called lies she told were part of her desire to appear attractive to those around her. She would create her own world where she was the centre of attention. Our 'psychiatrist with knobs on' was enthralled by her, wanting to know more about her particular approach to living.

The music which Martina selected for her Zumba classes was carefully considered. Martina had been interested in some research coming out of Brighton University on the importance of rhythms affecting brain waves. Apparently steady rhythms could allow the mind to relax, bringing the left and right hand hemispheres together making feelings more coherent. The quantum vibrations in brain neurons could affect individuals and help merge shared feelings. Martina knew that music could affect and energise people. Now she was consciously trying to do two things via the music she chose for her Zumba classes. First, to calm herself and move her chaotic mind towards a more tranquil stance. Secondly, to use music, singing and movement, to allow her to link with those she needed in her life. Musical entrainment would allow for cohesion and bonding to take place, as respiration and heart rates became synchronised. She could use music to help he get closer to those people who she needed. People who could fulfil her needs. The moment her new mark stroked her hair, Martina knew that she had chosen the correct music. The music Martina had selected for her Zumba classes had cast its spell.

Martina and her newly acquired psychiatrist quickly became enmeshed within each other, both wanting a closeness and both needing each other sexually. Their initial meetings were exceptional. Though both, whilst enjoying the halcyon days of a new romantic involvement, recognised that such perfect synchronicity could not last. Cracks would appear and disillusionment was bound to set in. The period of perfection would soon be replaced, quickly heralding the end of the affair. Martina knew this because it had happened to her so many times before. So many people had let her down. She had experienced so many broken liaisons. Her psychiatrist knew because her understanding of psychological concepts like love-bombing and splitting proved that the unrealistic perfect picture Martina had of her would soon be destroyed by reality. The moment the fantasy which Martina had created in her mind became even slightly tarnished, Martina would have to split, and end the affair. Splitting was a devastating experience for both partners. But, for the time being, during this initial stage of love-bombing, they were both enjoying the ride.

Martina had no idea of the thoughts which were surrounding her new conquest. She was delighting in the excitement of being with an older and intelligent psychiatrist who treated her as an equal and accepted her behaviour without question. On the other hand her psychiatrist, whilst enjoying the fun of her newly acquired princess could not remove the phrase which was circling her head … 'There is no health without mental health.'

Martina's plan of action was working. She enjoyed her classes at the gym and her supply needs were being met. She was still renting the windowless room in the small hotel by the station. She needed to move into better accommodation. She began looking.

Soon Friday came around and she was due to take an eleven o'clock class at the gym. She knew her psychiatrist would be there. They could easily play in the showers following the class. Martina felt more comfortable. Knowing that she was able to be assured that her sexual needs would be fulfilled was a comfort to her. She had enough stuff, to keep her happy too. She would smoke it regularly. It helped calm her and take the edge off her strained emotions. Life was beginning to look promising in London. She seemed to be able to get everything she needed in a small area of the city. Her medication was beginning to run out but she thought her psychiatrist would be able to help her obtain more. She was as content as she could be, given her agitated mind and her anxious way of being.

It was ten o'clock on a cloudy morning, when she was walking towards the gym. As she left the main thoroughfare she saw her current male squeeze beckoning her from across the road. She did not want to see him. He was out on the street. He may not be clean. She only really wanted to get close to him when they were showering. If they were in the shower she could be certain that he was clean. She carried on walking and tried to pretend she had not seen him. He became distraught, knowing she had seen him but was ignoring him. He would not be ignored. He ran across the road towards her, calling her name. She saw him coming towards her.

'Don't let him touch me. I won't be able to bear it if he touches me,' went through her head.

Too late, he had grabbed her by the arm and was pulling her towards him. She froze. She was unable to speak or to move. He, not realising her dismay, began telling her that there may be trouble at the gym for her. He had heard the manager on the phone, telling a friend that a detective would be visiting the gym on Friday to question the new member of staff. He did not know what about, but it seemed quite serious.

'What have you done?' he asked Martina jokingly. 'Have you robbed a bank or murdered someone?'

Martina became unfrozen. She wrenched herself away from his grasp and without a word began walking away from him towards the main station and the crowds of commuters. She needed to escape. She walked swiftly, leaving him bemused on the pavement. He did not follow. He was confused by her actions. He then began to wonder. Maybe she really had done something awful. If there was nothing to fear surely she would have just continued to the gym and seen the detective. She could have answered any questions and put everybody's mind at rest. But no, she had chosen to walk away. To walk fast. To walk as fast as she could away from the gym. She must have done something wrong.

He was left standing on the pavement wondering just what she had done. A few minutes later when he had gathered his composure, he walked towards the gym. After changing and doing some uninspired press-ups he noticed the manager talking to a man. They were either side of the reception desk and neither looked happy. Martina had not arrived.

The manager was upset because he had twelve eager women ready to begin the advertised Zumba class and no one to take it. Metod was frustrated because he had not found his prey. The two men began to argue. Metod was sure that the manager had warned Martina. The manager was sure that he hadn't. The two continued to argue as twelve disgruntled women collected their belongings and left the gym, some requesting a refund on the fees they had already paid.

Metod calmed down, trying to consider how he could salvage the situation. Whether he could find any snippets of information which would help him find her. He looked at the women leaving the gym.

'Did any of you know the trainer called Tina?' he asked.

The women continued walking towards the door, still grumbling about the class being cancelled without any prior notification. One woman turned round, scanning the others.

'I don't know if it's any use but Tina was friendly with the older woman, the woman who was the psychiatrist. I think she was called Pat. But neither of them has turned up today.'

Metod turned to the manager.

'Do you know the woman psychiatrist called Pat? Do you have her details?'

The manager looked at his screen. Yes, he had the name and address of the woman in question. He wrote the information on the back of a flyer advertising 'aromatherapy for those under stress', and handed it to Metod.

Metod did not thank the manager; he was still annoyed and was not convinced that the manager had not warned Martina of his visit. He left the gym and walked to the main road. A taxi was soon hailed and Metod was transported to the address of the psychiatrist.

The flat was in a large block overlooking a car park. Obviously for those 'over fifty five'. The taxi was paid and Metod walked towards the entrance. He pressed the number of the flat into the wall mounted entry box. Almost immediately a voice answered.

'Can I help you?'

Metod explained who he was and requested that he had entry so that he could continue their conversation in private. The owner of the dismembered voice was not happy to let him in. She tried to suggest that he visit the local police station. She asserted that she had no complaints about the gym or anyone at the gym. He then told the voice that he was looking for a trainer called Tina who worked at the gym but had disappeared. This sentence was the open sesame to the doors locking system. 'Click', the door was released. He quickly turned the handle and entered the building.

The lift took him to the third floor where he found the psychiatrist named Pat, standing at her open front door ready to greet him.

'Has something happened to Tina? Is she alright? Why are you looking for her?'

The questions tumbled from our anxious psychiatrist and across the hallway as Metod moved from the lift towards her.

They were soon sitting at her dining table. She was breathing heavily and obviously very concerned. He realised that she was more involved with Tina than he had at first thought.

She explained that her washing machine had broken down and she had been forced to await the arrival of the mechanics. That was why she had not attended the class. They sat together talking for over an hour. Despite asking all the relevant questions, at the end of their time together,

Metod was no wiser than when he had entered the building. The psychiatrist had no idea where Tina lived, nor any telephone link. She had only known her a short time and they had only met at the gym. She explained that Tina had seemed a friendly soul, in need of motherly guidance, which she had offered. The woman told Metod that she would often pick up stray young women who seemed lost in the big city. She felt sorry for them. She did not mention the fun she had had with Tina in the showers, or that she had observed certain personality traits, which might be deemed questionable. Pat was obviously used to concealing much, both professionally and personally. Metod was talking to a closed and unresponsive professional.

Eventually Metod left. He was getting nowhere. He had lost Martina. He decided that his only action now was to watch the gym in case she returned.

He found another taxi and returned to the roads around the gym. He would not tell the manager what he intended to do. For three days Metod stayed in the vicinity of the gym, just watching those going in and out. Martina did not show. After three days he rang his boss.

'Come home,' was his boss's response.

'We can't waste any more time or money on looking for this woman. We will just close the case and forget about the glasses. It was an unfortunate accident. Let's leave it at that.'

Metod was used to feeling frustrated. He often had to deal with situations which proved to be either unfathomable or simply unreal. Police work is challenging. The public can be exasperating. Metod could live with confusion and disappointment. However, he would usually try to mitigate any situations where he had made mistakes or misread intentions. He thought back to Mark's death. He felt sorry for the landlady. He had liked Sonia. At the back of his mind he had been concerned about his treatment of her. He had been forced to deceive her when he had taken the room in the house where Mark had lived. He disliked not being straight-forward. He had never really wanted to be involved in any undercover work. He wanted to be a straightforward, honest policeman. The type of policeman parents tell their children about. Someone who you can trust. Someone who can sort things out. Someone who upholds the laws of the land. His idea of himself had been compromised during the early part of his investigation when he lived with Mark. He needed to try to make amends. In order to do this he decided that he would visit the Cotswolds before he returned to Slovakia. He needed to see Sonia and apologise to her.

The next morning he was on a train heading for Cheltenham, with a large bunch of flowers purchased at Paddington Station. After arriving at Cheltenham station a taxi transported him to Sonia's house. He told the taxi to wait outside; he would not be long. He rang the bell and was soon smiling at his ex-landlady.

Sonia was her usual polite self, despite being very sur-prised to find him standing on her doorstep. She invited him in, offered tea and biscuits and sat to listen to the expla-nation for his unexpected visit. She had never felt comfort-able with him, whether he was called Tom or Metod. She was ill at ease being with him. Today was no exception. Despite his attempts to apologise for the deception, for the lies he had fed her, and the false references he had provided, she still seemed distant and suspicious. The flowers, though accepted, did little to sweeten her demeanour.

Metod realised that his explanations were failing to penetrate her cold expression. They made strained, idle conversation. She did not like him. They continued talking for while. Metod explained that the so called Enchantress had not been found. Sonia asked,

'Do you think that really Jo really was enchanted? Was there something magical going on?'

Metod laughed. 'No I don't believe in that sort of thing. It's all just silly gobbledygook! However I did find a strange sort of talisman in Jo's room. Look I have kept it. I don't really know what it is or what to do with it. I just sort of keep it for good luck.'

Metod put his hand in his pocket and pulled out the strange bead tied to ribbon, he had removed from Jo's flat. Sonia recognised it immediately. It was exactly the same as Mark's necklace she had secreted in her desk drawer.

'Oh, it's very pretty. I make necklaces. If you don't want it would you mind if I had it?'

Metod did not care whether she had it or not, but in the light of his previous lies to her and his deception, he did feel he owed her something. He reached across and put the bead in her hand.

'Thank you,' she smiled.

He stood to leave. Just as he was moving from the lounge into the hall she said,

'The coroner was a real support to me during that awful time. Some months after Mark's cremation he rang me, saying that there were two people from Africa wanting to meet with me and talk about Mark. I had had enough by then. I told the coroner that I knew nothing about Mark, nor his work, nor his life. I refused to see them.'

'You did the right thing,' was Metod's reply. Knowing the work of the American Intelligence Agency and the British Government Intelligence Agency, Metod realised that perhaps the 'two people from Africa' were still trying to discover how much she knew about Mark's work. He also thought they may have been trying to implicate Sonia in Mark's life in some way. Either way, it was best for her that she distanced herself from any further enquiries or involvements.

Whilst finishing the tea she had made, Sonia realised that she neither needed nor wanted Metod aka Tom to apologise to her. She wanted nothing more to do with him. Her initial feelings of dislike were being reinforced, however much he apologised or offered her flowers. Her mind was made up. She did not like him.

Metod sensed Sonia's coldness. He had achieved his objective … to apologise. He stood up, thanked her for the tea and left Sonia's house for good. The taxi was still outside. He got in and was soon on his way to Cheltenham station. It was the first stage in his return to Bratislava.

Sonia closed her front door. She knew what she wanted to do with the strange black bead hanging from the gros-grain ribbon. She sighed as she walked towards her study, open the desk drawer and took out Mark's nut necklace. She placed the two necklaces side by side in her left hand, stroking them gently with her right hand, knowing that they belonged together.

Sonia was an interesting mix of down-to-earth practicality and unsubstantiated spiritual concerns. She felt she had been drawn into considering the world of magic and occultism from an early age. Despite her Protestant upbringing and her practical predisposition there was a part of her that was not really of this world. Her father had had the capacity for faith healing and other members of her family had been psychic. She had often been told that she too was psychic.

On the morning of her father's death he had frightened her by telling her that she had healing powers. Sonia did not want to acknowledge anything other than immediate reality. Like Metod, she tried to see it all as gobbledygook. She tried but did not succeed. There was always that slight apprehension. Supposing there was something in it? Supposing it was not gobbledygook?

Sonia had decided what to do with the two necklaces she now had in her possession. She had visited the beautiful Tuscan town of Sansepolcro during a summer holiday in Italy. There she had come across an interesting herbalist museum, celebrating the therapeutic power of herbs and the relationship between man and plants. She had discovered the importance of trees. Apparently a man called William Williams of Gloucestershire had written a book in 1660 called *Occult Physick*, explaining the magical power of trees. The rowan tree had been thought to be sacred and able to dispel spells and witchcraft. If an elixir of green berries (they had to be green), if an elixir of green berries was taken, any spells would be broken.

Sonia put on her coat and walked across the road to the house where Mark had died. Despite being newly renovated, it was still empty. Taking her key she entered and walked up the stairs to Mark's freshly decorated room. She looked through the window at the rowan tree which grew in the garden below. As her eyes lifted towards the blue sky she said,

'My blessings are with you, Mark. And with your Peter Pan.'

Slowly she left the room, descended the stairs and headed towards the back door, where she entered into the garden. The two necklaces hung from her left hand. She carefully picked two berries from the rowan tree and rubbed them against the black kukui nuts, hopefully dissipating any possible fascination of evil spirits or spells. She then hung both necklaces side by side on the highest branch she could reach. The rowan tree swayed in the warm breeze as the necklaces danced side by side. She said a prayer and again asked Mark's forgiveness for losing his ashes. Mark's hill looked down upon the scene. The kukui nut necklaces were now able to remain alongside each other moving in perfect synchronicity, just looking towards the hill. Sonia knew that she had done all she could to ensure the comfort of both Mark and Jo as they continued on their journey towards their shared eternity.

She sighed as she left the garden and returned to her own house. Instinctively she headed towards the kitchen and the tupperware container that concealed her emergency store of ginger biscuits covered in thick dark chocolate. She had convinced herself on numerous occasions that the ginger was good for her. Soon there were four fewer biscuits in the container and Sonia's sugar levels were heading for the ceiling.

As his plane touched down in Slovakia, Metod knew he was in a sad mood. He had not foreseen that his trip to London might not get the results he desired. After easily clearing customs, he went straight to his office in police headquarters. No one spoke or mentioned his trip. Everyone knew he would be upset at his failure. They shared his disappointment. Martina could not be found, neither in Slovakia nor in London. The Enchantress with the green glasses seemed to be an enigmatic enchantment. No one could find her. Jo's death was duly recorded as an unfortunate accident and the case was finally closed. Metod had failed.

CHAPTER FIFTEEN

EVERY ENDING IS A NEW BEGINNING – COVID ERA

'Inch by inch I conquered the inner terrain I was born with. Bit by bit I reclaimed the swamp in which I'd languished. I gave birth to my infinite being but I had to wrench myself out of me with forceps.'

Fernando Pessoa, *The Book of Disquiet*

'I cannot bear it. I must get away. I must find a new me. I must escape.' Martina ached as her overwrought mind threw yet more confusion into her world.

The area around St Pancras station was overflowing with a deluge of dripping bodies, all trying to evade the dismal rain which drizzled towards them. Martina rushed from the grasping arms of her current, soon to become her ex-beau and headed towards the crowds and the anonymity of the station's surroundings. She needed to get away from his overbearing interruptions and away from any inquisitive individuals asking to see her at the gym. For the first time since leaving Slovakia she felt afraid. Her normal state of mind was one of continuous anxiety and concern, but she was feeling something different now. She would usually try to offer herself supportive inner mantras to calm her feelings. She would say,

'You are fine. There is nothing to be anxious about. Stay calm. Breathe deeply. No one is going to hurt you. Everything will be OK.'

Sadly, today she could not find the words she needed. Her soothing words had been crushed by a tidal wave of aggressive sounds which held thorns that scraped her consciousness. Pain rattled round her throbbing skull.

'It's all exploding. Get away from the danger. You are in harm's way. Don't get caught. Run as fast as you can. Hide again. Find somewhere where you can't be found. You are in danger now, this very minute. Get away. Get away fast.'

Martina left the hustle of the station and headed towards the small room in the cheap hotel. She threw all her clothes and belongings into her suitcase and a large plastic carrier bag with 'Homesense' written in large letters along the side. She looked at the bag. She knew she had to find a home. She had the sense enough to know that she needed to find a home soon. She tried to translate 'homesense' into Slovakian. There was no equivalent. She picked up her phone and began searching for rooms to rent. There were two which looked interesting. She had already telephoned one of them and arranged a viewing at the weekend. She decided to go now. She needed to move from the hotel as soon as possible. She did not want anyone from the gym being able to find her.

After checking that there was no one on duty at the front desk, she quickly left the building. Knowing she would not be returning, she justified her leaving without settling her bill by the fact that it was not her fault that she had to leave. She had been forced by others wanting to see her, wanting to ask her questions. It was their fault that she had to leave so quickly, and it was their fault that she didn't pay her bill.

She had time to settle her bill, but she chose not to. Her underdeveloped conscience was soon overcome by her own brand of justification. She would not pay.

Although she had no idea who was looking for her at the gym, she did know that she needed to remain anonymous. She did not want any links with Slovakia or her family or anyone who knew anything about her. She had wanted to disappear when she left Slovakia. Now she knew she needed to change who she was. Her new life had to begin with her as a new and untraceable woman.

She had noticed a beauty parlour and hairdressers near the station. Carrying her one suitcase and her large bag she went into the shop asking if they could fit her in for a colour and a treatment. There were six girls and one man working. The man agreed saying that as long as she did not mind having a trainee to colour her hair, under his guidance of course, then they could fit her in immediately. Martina was relieved.

Two hours later she emerged with her shoulder length hair teased gently into tight ringlets. The colour had changed from auburn to a mixture of deep brown, mahogany and purple, with pink streaks. It looked magnificent. She was very pleased as the trainee held up the small mirror allowing her to view the back of her colourful coiffeur. She had also had a manicure and a pedicure. Her nails were now covered in a vibrant green varnish. She felt delighted with her new persona. No one would recognise her now.

She thanked the staff, paid her extortionate bill and started to leave the building. Just as she was going through the door, the trainee called her back. Martina froze. What was wrong? Why was she being called back? What had she done? He fear gave way to her innate curiosity as she managed to turn her head towards the trainee, expecting some rebuke or criticism.

'You look so good, but there is one thing missing. Please accept this gift from us all. It's OK, the manager said I can give it to you.'

The trainee smiled as she moved towards the stricken Martina and handed her a lipstick. It was the same shade of green as her nails. Smiles always worked for Martina. She always wanted, indeed needed smiles to help her manage her life. Smiles could hide everything.

She smiled back, as her composure returned and her mask of polite superficiality hid her confusion.

'Oh, that's so kind of you. It will really go well with my new image. Thank you so much.'

Martina looked in the mirror, placed her bags on the floor, and applied the green lipstick. The newly transformed Martina was looking ever more exceptional. She was pleased.

On leaving the beauty parlour she walked to the river. Actually she glided to the river. She felt so good. She was beginning her new life. She so enjoyed starting again. She was amazed to see that people passing her were smiling at her. She smiled back, giving them her best smile. Smiles were so important to her. She remembered a song her parents had played when she was little. She opened Google on her phone. The old song, 'Give Me a Smile' now recreated by Scarlette Fever purred around her. She loved that song. The words caressed her disturbed mind. They spoke just to her. She was expecting other worlds to begin for her. She knew the past had passed and she wanted the stillness in her soul that the song promised. She had the courage to see how limitless she was. She was hopeful that everything would be going her way. She needed things to go her way. She needed the universe to be on her side. Her inner turmoil, pain and constant confusion necessitated her outer world being supportive and calm.

She put her bags down by her side and peered over the stone wall into the swirling metallic greys of the river below. She would find new digs, she would find a new job, she would find new lovers, and she would find new supply. Her life would be good. She sent her wishes into the river and watched them float downstream.

As her thoughts were drifting towards some faraway sea she remembered the things she had in her overstuffed rucksack. She opened the zip and carefully took out her two passports. The newly created Martina would not need her old passport. She would be Martina Green from now on. She felt slight apprehension as she remembered her signature green glasses which she had lost in the caves. Her replacement pair glared back at her from the open bag. The new Martina would not be needing them anymore. With one swift gesture she threw her old Slovakian passport and her spare green glasses into the hungry waters. They floated downstream, following her thoughts towards a distant ocean. Gone. All that remained was the new Martina. After a short period of alteration in the beauty parlour and some adjustments by the riverside, Martina Green had emerged reborn.

Most newborns learn to walk before they can run. Martina Green was born running. Her first challenge was to escape from the area and find another place to live. She looked at her note pad. The address of the vacant room she had found was in south London. It was an area she did not know. It was far enough away from both the station and the gym to be safely left behind. She would not accidentally meet anyone from her initial stay in London. She could start again in south London.

London was magical. London could hide her. The city was vast and full of all sorts of people. Most people would rush to meet their own agendas. Most people would just be interested in their own worlds, not wanting nor caring about the worlds of those around them. London was bursting and overfull of non-caring, self indulgent individuals, rushing about their own business. Martina could easily get lost within its ever-increasing inward looking multitudes.

Two hours later she was getting out of a taxi at the first address she had written on the paper. In front of her was a large double fronted house, made of grey bricks and white triple-glazing. The road was busy; a main thoroughfare for traffic and pedestrians. The houses which lined either side of the road were squashed together, each one seeming to hold up the others as they lent upon each other for support. The front aspect of the house was flat and boring. There was no garden to the front, and the large entrance door was approached by two steps leading up from the grey pavement. With little enthusiasm Martina rang the bell. There was no response. No one came to the door. No one seemed to be home.

Martina, not knowing what to do next, sat on the doorstep and propped her luggage against the wall. She would wait. Eventually someone had to come. She took out her recently acquired new phone and began to try to work out the 'Wordle' of the day. She found it a challenge. She hoped it would improve her English if she did a Wordle every day. Whilst she was sitting surrounded by her suitcase, her Homesense bag and her coat, she noticed three young women getting off the bus on the other side of the road. They were chatting and laughing. She put her phone away and watched them as they crossed the road and walked towards her, still chatting and laughing. On reaching the step they stopped and loomed over her, the shortest member of the trio asked.

'What are you doing sitting on our doorstep?'

Martina immediately realised that these were the women who she hoped she would be sharing a house with in the not too distant future.

'I rang last night. About the room to let. I thought I had a viewing tonight. I must have got muddled as I have been seeing so many rooms,' she lied.

The women looked at each other. The shortest one took the lead again.

'Well, we don't know anything about a viewing today, but we do have a spare room to let. Are you the woman who is supposed to come at the weekend? Would you like to come in and see it now?'

Martina said she was the woman, and apologised for getting the days mixed up. She stood up and they all entered the building.

The women had been trying to let the fourth room for some time. They were eager to find a new flatmate as the bills were becoming too much for them to share between just the three of them. They led Martina into the large front room. The room was freshly decorated. Everything looked very clean. The furniture had all been painted white. There were three tall windows and an oversized wardrobe like cupboard with two doors which, when opened, formed a small kitchenette.

Martina looked around. The room seemed acceptable. The kitchenette in the cupboard was useful. It held a sink, a small fridge and a microwave. The women then showed her the bathroom which had an integral toilet. Immediately Martina realised that the sharing of a bathroom would cause her major problems. She could not share with the other women. She could not share a bathroom. She also noticed a small toilet with a sink at the end of the hall adjacent to the room they were offering her. Immediately her quick thinking allowed her to consider a plan which could be workable. She would offer to pay the women so much a month if they would allow her to use the one separate toilet next to her room. They would then have to use the bathroom or the outside toilet in the backyard which they had mentioned earlier. If she could negotiate having her own toilet and sink then it would be a feasible solution. She outlined her plan to the women. They did not seem to be concerned about sharing a toilet, especially if it gave them extra cash. Soon it was agreed. Martina would have the single toilet all to herself. Martina had got what she wanted. She liked to get what she wanted. Compromise was not something she usually considered.

Seeing her two large bags the women wondered why she had brought so much luggage. They asked her. Her reply was convincing. Her act was faultless.

'My boyfriend has thrown me out,' she spluttered.

'He had already moved his new girlfriend in when I got home. My bags were just left in the hall. He had thrown all my stuff into them and even flung my books into the front garden. They were all sodden and ruined. His new girlfriend just watched as I left. She was so beautiful and much younger than me. Obviously he wanted a new model.'

After her emotional explanation they all felt very sorry for her. They knew how it felt to be dropped and replaced.

Obviously she could not go home and she had nowhere else to stay. She continued, telling them that she hoped she could move in immediately. She blew her nose and continued to snivel into her tissue.

The three kind women offered her comforting words. They had all had boyfriend troubles so they could identify with Martina's problems. Nods of heads allowed them to tell her that of course she could move in. The room was hers.

Martina thanked them, adding that references were on their way. They would be able to have them at a later date, when she had got them from Slovakia. One of the women then asked, 'You don't have any pet rats, tarantulas or any other animals do you?'

They all laughed as Martina looked bewildered. The question had relieved the tension in the air.

Apparently one of the previous women viewing the room had wanted to bring pet rats and eight tarantulas into the house. She had explained that the rats were 'totally lovable' and 'happy little creatures'. She had amazed them all by recounting how the tarantulas would shed their furry skins, which she kept. On being asked what they ate she gave a detailed description of how she would feed them crickets or cockroaches, quickly adding that mealworms were another alternative, but she didn't like worms so she never bought them. The tarantulas would hold the crickets or cockroaches in their fangs, releasing venom as they sucked the life out of their victims. Our prospective flat mates had been horrified. Subsequently they had told her that sadly the room had already been taken.

Martina grimaced as she assured them she had no insects or creatures, nor would she ever bring anything 'alive' into her room as she needed clean surroundings. The women seemed pleased with her response. So it was agreed. She would move in directly. She was pleased. All she had to do now was to find work in the vicinity.

Martina Green settled into her new home very quickly. She bought a new white clock which she hung on the wall. She put a padlock on her toilet door. She shopped for bananas and tins. She would only eat from tins. If you opened the food yourself you could be assured that it was uncontaminated. She always had bananas and tins on hand in case she felt hungry. Sometimes she would have Coke from a can too. Bottles were dangerous as bottles could be opened and resealed. Nasties could be put into bottles. No one could open a can and reseal it. Cans were safe.

Slowly she opened her suitcase. Her possessions were few. Clothes were all folded neatly alongside a transparent plastic bag containing various articles of gold jewellery which had previously belonged to her mother. Tucked between her tee shirts and sports gear was an image of a mandala. The glass was framed by an intricately carved white wooden surround. Martian knew that Buddhist mandalas represented an ideal universe. How she longed to live in an ideal universe. Mandalas would aid purification and healing. For many years she had contemplated her mandala, hoping it would help with her anxiety and stress. She hung the framed image on the wall opposite the white clock. She was pleased with her new room.

At last she was alone in her new haven, surrounded by her few possessions. She sat in the large turquoise velvet armchair, closed her eyes and listened to Julia Brennan singing 'Inner Demons'. She hoped that she had left her inner demons in Slovakia. She prayed that any demons would not find their way to her new home in England. She wanted to be free of them and live an angelic English existence. She prayed that Julia's angels, knowing that life was hurtful and unfair, would take away all her pain and fear. She slipped something from her rucksack into her mouth, swallowed and then lit a cigarette. Gradually she entered a hidden world where she could find escape. Sleep followed her.

When she awoke she felt settled in her new accommodation. After being initially friendly to her flat mates she retreated into her self-imposed secrecy. She did not want to disclose anything about herself to her newly acquired 'mates'. However, on knowing that she wanted to find work they had knocked on her door one evening. They suggested that she join them at the local factory, making child push-chairs and scooters. All three worked there with various shifts. They knew the manager was always looking for new staff.

Martina thanked them politely,

'I really want to be working with something related to dance or swimming. I could even consider involvement in other sports activities. Thank you so much for thinking of me but I don't think so.'

She knew she had to exercise. She knew that she had to shower. She knew she had to maintain a daily routine of movement to help her manage her levels. Movement and physical exhaustion was necessary to her well being. She was soothed by physical activity. On the other hand she could not think of anything more distasteful than working with her chatty housemates in an unclean environment surrounded by all sorts of odd individuals. The very thought of entering such an establishment made her feel quite nauseous.

For two weeks Martina scoured the internet and the local papers. No luck. There did not seem to be any work out there. She was beginning to worry. She feared that her money would run out. She had already exchanged some of her mother's jewellery for cash. She was beginning to have nightmares again. Her head would throb as she tried to push any demons down into her body. She wondered if the universe was playing tricks with her again. Her self soothing, from the supply hidden in her rucksack, was no longer effective. She put on her music. Even that did not help. She was beginning to enter a world where control would be lost. She was heading towards yet another downward spiral which was digging into her consciousness.

As she huddled in her bed one afternoon, wondering how to navigate her unruly thoughts and erratic mood swings, one of her housemates came home from her session at the factory and banged joyfully on her door. Martina never invited anyone into her room. It needed to stay clean. However, she could not ignore the banging. She hid her annoyance under her smiley false mask, opened her door and stepped into the hall, necessitating the woman who had been banging to step backwards.

'Hey Martina, you won't believe this, but one of the part time blokes came into the cafeteria at the factory for lunch. He is doing a course at the university and he was talking about the new sports complex that had just opened. He said that they were looking for instructors. It sounds as if it might be just what you are looking for. Here, I got the name of the manager and his phone number for you.'

She thrust a screwed-up piece of paper into Martina's hands.

'Thank you so much. I'll ring him directly.'

Martina turned and retreated into her room, closing the door behind her. She straightened the crumpled piece of paper and stared at the numbers in front of her. The thought of working in a Sports Centre appealed to her. She knew that the physicality of the work and the release of all her juggling nerve endings would help sooth her being. She knew she needed to move. She knew she needed to work. Maybe the universe was going to help her again. Maybe it had forgiven her for all her previous transgressions. She bowed to the mandala as she slowly fed the numbers into her phone …

Two days later, after a demanding interview, she was offered the job at the newly opened University Sports Centre, teaching Zumba and synchronised swimming. The universe was on her side again.

Life was going well for Martina Green. She had found somewhere to live. She had successfully got a job in a new, clean Sports Centre. She would be able to shower as often as she wished. All she needed to do now was to find credulous individuals to supply her daily needs. She needed soothing. She needed supply and she needed sex. She anticipated that the University Sports Centre would be full of empathetic, gullible people who would be delighted to be love bombed by her gorgeousness.

The day arrived for her to start her new job. She arrived early, thinking she would wander round the buildings before signing in. She walked into the Sports Centre and moved towards the large hall which held the impressive indoor climbing complex. There were five good looking bodies moving up the vertical wall spaces. Each body followed a different course, directed by the colour coding of the various rocks and outcrops which were scattered across the extensive and challenging climbing network.

Martina looked at the bodies. She was searching for her new mark. Singles were her choice with women, but married men would always be ready to have some fun and they usually could find money easily. Married men were generally the most available and like her, they always sought secrecy. Her eyes moved from one body to the next, looking for wedding rings, and wondering who would be the most suitable.

Miley Cyrus began singing 'The Climb' over the music system. Martina loved the song; she joined in singing at the top of her voice. Like the song, she too felt her life was always in turmoil. Each day she had to confront new mountains to climb, new challenges to overcome. She could be thrust into mental depths with no understanding of when or why. She was at the mercy of her mind. Anxiety could permeate her thoughts. When she tried to find ways to climb from the deep crevasses which lay below her, she was always anxious and fearful, thinking she would fail. She knew she had to maintain control. She could not afford to lose control. Now she felt she had control. Now she could sing with Miley.

As she looked at the bodies above her she hoped that the universe would help her find what she was seeking. The bodies looked down, wondering who was making the noise. Martina looked up.

Just as she was about to consciously consider which of the fit bodies balanced high above her would fulfil her needs, the unreliable universe withdrew its recent assistance. Martina felt an internal tsunami flush across her shoulders and down her back. Suddenly she sensed fearful fissures open beneath her as a deluge of her demons reached to pull her down into the swamp below. She fell as the mountain terrain tumbled around her and her climb ended. Life was changing yet again. Life was not good.

The music stopped and a newsflash transmitted from the speakers, heralded the start of a new era. Everyone listened attentively, not believing what they were hearing. Martina tried to calm her breathing. Anxiety cloaked her mind and body. Emotions jarred her being. Fear furrowed into her pores. Something was happening ... but not just to her.

Slowly

Everyone, including Martina, felt the universe withdraw its support

Fear and confusion roamed the streets and fields alike

Others, all others, became threatening

Life became endangered – Life became fearful – Life became unbearable

A dispassionate and impotent universe contemplated from afar

as the Covid pandemic hit the world

EVERYTHING CHANGED

The quavering voice of the Sports Centre manager screeched from the sound system, giving everyone clear instructions. The climbers slowly descended in silence. The Sports Centre was quickly emptied. Everyone left.

The following days, Martina Green, with emerald nails hidden by orange plastic gloves and green lipstick shrouded by flimsy blue facemasks, struggled to evade the proliferating germs which seemed to be attacking the populous. No one knew what was happening. People were being taken to hospital, many never came out. The news channels seemed contradictory and confused. Keeping away from others was deemed the best solution for avoiding the virus which roamed the streets.

The following weeks saw the Sports Centre shut down due to Covid regulations. Lockdowns ensued. A solitary Martina had to remain isolated in her room. She wondered when she would find her new mark. She needed sex. She needed money. She needed supply. The universe had abandoned her yet again. She felt the virus called Covid was targeting her personally. It was disrupting her plans. It was stopping her do the things she needed to do.

Martina Green's new life had been changed forever. Her plans had been thwarted. She looked out of her window at the abandoned street below. No cars, no people, no noise. The whole scene was locked into a still tableau of coldness and confusion. Not even a sprinkling of rain to tickle her window panes.

She threw her coffee mug at the white wall as she screamed out loud. Strands of coffee ran towards the floor, staining the pristine whiteness. Her anger was acute as she reached for her small kitchen knife. Contemplating the thunderbolt tattoo on her wrist, she collapsed into a sobbing ball of raw energy. She knew her future in England was being devastated by this random virus. How she hated the virus. How she hated the Sports Centre being closed. How she hated all those partners who had let her down. Thoughts of Jo entered her mind. How she hated Jo.

One sudden movement and pain ensued. Her curled up ball of body parts pulsated with sobs as her inner demons pulled her further towards them. Her new beginnings had been hi-jacked. It could only get worse.

Her subsequent screams were quelled. Her body became numb as it tried to regulate her emotions and stop her overwhelming self hatred. Her mind clawed at a new understanding. She hoped that when the physical pain subsided it could temper her emotional trauma. She hoped it would eventually offer her some sort of relief.

The last thing Martina saw was the Buddhist mandala on the wall. It was now covered with coffee stains. The caption underneath read,

'EVERY ENDING IS A NEW BEGINNING'

Martina closed her eyes, dropped the knife, and pulled her gaping wrist towards her chest. Silence and stillness were all that was left in the room.

She passed out.

(If you want to discover what happened to Martina and explore her dramatic and extraordinary experiences in England during Covid time, you may like to read the sequel to this story called *Lockdown Angel*, also by Carroll Clarke. Proceeds from both books will be given to mental health charities. Thank you for your support.)

THE SONGS

Chapter One

Chapter Two

Chapter Three

Chapter Four

Chapter Five

Chapter Six

Kelsey Ballerini. . . . . Peter Pan

R.E.M.. . . . . Everybody Hurts

Chopin. . . . . Nocturn in E Flat Major

Simon and Garfunkel. . . . . . The Sound of Silence

Heleentje Van Capelle . . . . . Naar de Speeltuin (Never
Never Land)

Chapter Seven

Martha and the Vandellas. . . Dancing in the Street

Ed Sheeran. . . . . Perfect

Camila Cabello . . . . Don't Go Yet

Supertramp . . . . Give a Little Bit

Chapter Eight

Lighthouse Family . . . . Lifted

Christina Perri . . . . A Thousand Years

Metallica . . . . Nothing Else Matters

Marina Lin. . . . . This Is What Depression
Feels Like

Chapter Nine

Sigrid . . . . Bring Me The Horizon –
Bad Life

Noelle Johnson. . . . . Broken

Westlife . . . . Alone Together

Joy Division . . . . She's Lost Control

Chapter Ten

Lunar Year . . . . Boys Will Cry

Tina Turner . . . . I Don't Want to Lose You

The Beatles . . . . I'm Looking Through You

Natalie Cole . . . . Smile

Chapter Eleven

Beth Crowley . . . . Perfect Doesn't Last

Emeli Sandé . . . . Read All About It

Chapter Twelve

Justin Bieber . . . . Ghost

Brent Morgan . . . . The Fixer

Chapter Thirteen

Ed Sheeran . . . . Bad Habits

Chapter Fifteen

Scarlette Fever . . . . Give Me a Smile (A Tribute
to John Barry)

Julia Brennan . . . . Inner Demons

Miley Cyrus . . . . The Climb

FINAL COGITATIONS

Lockdown Angel, published January 2022, noted that 'mood and anxiety disorders, personality disorders and the increase of psychosis appear to be more prevalent during periods of extended stress and uncertainty'. The book focused on the Covid pandemic as initiating a worldwide period of 'stress and uncertainty'. Two months later, March 2022, heralded inter-continental aggression adding yet another dimension to our shared experiences, with stress and uncertainty being highlighted regularly on numerous news channels. The Autumn of 2022 gave rise to much political and social turbulence.

Life experience has proved to us all that trauma is more widely experienced than just in medical settings. Trauma is a wound, a deep hurt and its pain may continue for a lifetime. Most childhood experiences affect our adult feelings and subsequent behaviours. We currently live in a world surrounded by traumatic transgressions.

Feeling safe is a basic need, but sadly safety is being challenged daily. We are forced to encounter new variants, new uncertainties, new stressors, new challenges to the world order. In short, new and increased reasons to focus on our mental health. Managing and maintaining our mental health must become a priority, both personally and globally. Understanding and expanding insights into the complexity and sheer wonder of our magnificent minds may be one way to help us feel safer and to help us better understand our own mental health and the mental health of those around us.

1) 'For our physiology to calm down, heal and grow we need a visceral feeling of safety. No doctor can write a prescription for friendship and love. These are complex and hard-earned capacities. You don't need a history of trauma to feel self-conscious or even panicked at a party with strangers – but trauma can turn the whole world into a gathering of aliens.'

'... almost all mental suffering involves either trouble in creating workable and satisfying relationships or difficulties in regulating arousal (as in the case of habitually becoming enraged, shut down, overexcited or disorganized). Usually a combination of both.'

Bessel Van de Kolk, *The Body Keeps the Score,* Penguin Books, 2014, pp. 92 and 91.

2) 'Depression is a mood disorder that involves a persistent feeling of sadness and loss of interest. It is different from the mood fluctuations that people regularly experience as a part of life.'

'Depression is the main cause of disability worldwide, according to the World Health Organization (WHO). It can affect adults, adolescents, and children.'

'The medical community does not fully understand the causes of depression. There are many possible causes, and sometimes, various factors combine to trigger symptoms. Factors that are likely to play a role include: genetic features, changes in the brain's neurotransmitter levels, environmental factors, psychological and social factors.'

'Aerobic exercise raises endorphin levels and stimulates the neurotransmitter norepinephrine, which is linked with mood. This may help relieve mild depression.'

From *Medical New Today*, Last medically reviewed on November, 22, 2019. www.medicalnewstoday.com.

3) 'Depression … is a common but serious mood disorder. It causes severe symptoms that affect how you feel, think, and handle daily activities, such as sleeping, eating or working.'

'Some forms of depression are slightly different, or they may develop under unique circumstances.

'The Centers for Disease Control and Prevention (CDC) has recognized that having certain mental disorders, including depression and schizophrenia, can make people more likely to get severely ill from Covid-19.'

From *National Institute of Mental Health* (NIMH) which is part of the National Institutes of Health (NIH), a component of the U.S. Department of Health and Human Services, 2022.

4) 'Depression is also smaller than you. Always, it is smaller than you, even when it feels vast. It operates within you, you do not operate within it. It may be a dark cloud passing across the sky but – if that is the metaphor – you are the sky. You were there before it. And the cloud can't exist without the sky, but the sky can exist without the cloud.'

Matt Haig, *Reasons to Stay Alive*, Canongate Books, 2015.

5) 'Schizoid personality disorder is a personality disorder characterized by a lack of interest in social relationships, a tendency toward a solitary or sheltered lifestyle, secretiveness, emotional coldness, detachment and apathy. Affected individuals may be unable to form intimate attachments to others and simultaneously possess a rich and elaborate but exclusively internal fantasy world.'

From Wikipedia, 'Schizoid Personality Disorder', Article. Last edited 26 November 2022 by Acire93.

6) 'The stages of limerence includes addictive type behaviour, thinking about the other 24 hrs a day, stress, heart palpitations, stomach anxiety and even intrusive thoughts. It's best described as an uncontrollable, overwhelming desire for someone.'

Charlotte Grainger, *Limerence v Love*, 2021.

7) The Priory group carried out research which found that

'Around 1 in 5 (21%) adults experienced some form of depression in early 2021.(27th Jan to 7th March) This is an increase since Nov 2020 and more than double that observed before the coronavirus (Covid 19) pandemic (10%).

'70% of people across the country would not reveal a mental health issue to work colleagues.'

www.priorygroup.com.

8) 'Limerence is a romantic attraction to another person that typically includes obsessive thoughts, fantasies

and a desire to either form or maintain a romantic relationship with a specific person. It's an all –consuming, involuntary state of romantic desire'.

From Zachary Zane, 'Is It Love, or Is It Limerence? Having an Obsessive, Overpowering Crush is an Actual Condition', *Men's Health*, 30 January 2020.

9) 'In the last analysis, learning how to transcend the ego involves nothing less than learning how to be open to love. Only love has the power to save us from ourselves. Until we learn to truly love ourselves and others – there can be no hope of lasing happiness or peace or redemption.'

'We are all blinded to the fullness and magnificence of our ultimate nature by the trance of our personality. Our true nature exists only now, in this very moment. It includes all the concerns and motivations of our personality while also transcending all of them.'

Richard Riso with Russ Hudson, *Personality Types*, Houghton Mifflin Company, New York, 1996, pp. 460 and 457.

10) 'The degree of aggressiveness expressed during an episode (of anger) is grossly out of proportion to any provocation or situational stress ... often genuine regret is expressed after the outburst.'

From Online article, 'Conditions > Impulse Control Disorders > Intermittent Explosive Disorders', *Psychology Today*. Reviewed by *Psychology Today* staff, 2022.

11) 'Schizoids are loners. Given the option, they invariably pursue solitary activities or hobbies. Inevitably, they prefer mechanical or abstract tasks and jobs that

require such skills. Many computer hackers, crackers, and programmers are schizoids, for instance – as are some mathematicians and theoretical physicists.'

From 'Schizoid Personality Disorder' in Sam Vaknin, *Personality Disorders Revisited*, 2013.

12) 'I think of schizoid personality disorder as the hidden disorder because most people with it are suffering very quietly.'

'The basic response that most people with SPD have to their social fears is to physically and emotionally distance themselves as much as possible from other people.'

'When I asked one of my schizoid clients what they would like me to tell people about schizoid personality disorder, she said "Tell them that they will never guess what we are really feeling from looking at us".'

Elinor Greenberg 'Understanding Narcissism – What Everyone Ought to Understand About Schizoid Personality Disorder' Posted 17 October 2020. www.psychologytoday.com.

13) 'Psychologists, anthropologists, ethnologists and sociologists who study behaviours struggle to understand why we are violent or murderous.'

'Animal behaviour is the product of emotion, instinct and reasoning.'

'91% of men and 84% of women have considered killing someone.'

Buss also suggests that the underlying issues surrounding murderous thoughts include;
- Unstable family relationships

- Cultural values
- Mental disorders

David Buss, Professor of Psychology at the University of Texas, surveyed 5,000 people in his book *The Murderer Next Door, Why the Mind is Designed to Kill.*

14) NHS 'Where to Get Help for Self-Harm'. www.nhs. uk, 23 July 2022. Next review 23 July 2023.

15) 'The Kukui (nut) is a transmitter and receiver that aligns to the la'a kea (love light) energy level, the auric field and all resonating factors. It is a powerful amplifier for sending love and light.'

Mary Kawena Pukui, 'Olelo No'eau', *Hawaiian Proverbs and Poetical Sayings*, Bishop Museum Press, 1983.

16)

Throughout the ages emeralds have been valued for both their beauty and their associations. They are the stone associated with Venus, and they represent truth, rebirth and love. The Incas and Aztecs worshipped them as gods. They are rarer than diamonds.

In ancient Egypt emeralds were viewed as symbolising eternal life and youth. Emeralds were placed on mummies to signify the eternal youth of the afterlife and to protect the limbs of the body.

The links between the human eye and the emerald has been recorded in many civilisations. It is believed to cure and sooth eyes or enhance vision. Nero is purported to have used an eye-glass made of transparent emeralds.

The colour emerald green is both brilliant and lethal. Originally the formula for emerald green contained arsenic and was therefore highly toxic. Those experiencing high levels of exposure would suffer from hallucinations and eventual arsenic poisoning. Death could occur.

Emeralds were also considered a magical stone, linking the earth to the universe, whilst fulfilling wishful thoughts and desires. One of the main properties associated with the stone is the ability to offer protection from spells and enchantments.

The poet, TS Eliot was reported to have had an addiction to cosmetics. He was purported to have worn green face powder and lipstick to enhance his appearance which, according to Clive Bell of the Bloomsbury Group, helped him to look more 'interesting and cadaverous'.

Dorothy wore green glasses when she visited Oz and travelled to the Emerald City. Indeed, the city was not made of emeralds, but the green glasses made the city appear green.

'Even with eyes protected by the green spectacles, Dorothy and her friends were at first dazzled by the brilliance of the wonderful city.'

Frank Baum, *The Wonderful Wizard of Oz*, 1900.

REFERENCES AND INFLUENCERS

Books and Articles

Barrie, James Matthew, *Peter Pan*, Puffin Classics, 2010

Baum, Frank, *The Wonderful Wizard of Oz*, Dover Children's Classics, 2015

Klein, R, *The Self in Exile*, Brunner/Mazel, 1995

McHugh, Paul R, *Try to Remember: Psychiatry's Clash Over Meaning, Memory and Mind*, 1/11/2008

Pessoa, Fernando, *The Book of Disquiet*, Random House, 2015

Penthrick, Wayne and Grant Sinnamon (eds), *The Psychology of Criminal and Antisocial Behavior: Victim and Offender Perspectives*. Chapter 16 'The Psychology of Adult Sexual Grooming'. Elsevier Science Publishing Co. Inc., 2017

Vaknin, Sam, *Malignant Self-Love: Narcissism Revisited*, 10th edition, 2015

Van Der Colk, Bessel, *The Body Keeps the Score: Mind, Brain and Body in the Transformation of Trauma*, Penguin Books, 2014

Videos and YouTube Posts, Online Articles

Cherry, Kendra. 'Repression as a Defense Mechanism', The Very Well Mind, 25 April 2021

Durvasula, Dr Ramani, 'The 5 Signs Someone Has Suffered Narcissistic Abuse' YouTube MedCircle, 10 January 2020

— 'What It's Like to Break Up with a Narcissist', 22 August 2020

— 'Signs you're healing from a narcissitic relationship', February 2022

Mancao, Alyssa, 'Seven Ways to Deal with Gaslighting, From a Therapist', Mindbodygreen, 16 April 2021

mind.org.uk, online article 'What is Self Harm?', May 2020

Vaknin, Sam, 'Why Narcissist Devalues YOU (Hint: Wants YOU "Dead")', December 2021

— 'Two Faces of Narcissistic Abuse: Disrespect From Shared Fantasy to Bargaining', November 2021

— 'Borderline Personality Disorder Reconceived', December 2021